The Exiled Prophet

The Exiled Prophet

SELECTED FICTION
BY NAJI DHAHER

Translated and Edited by

Hazza Abu Rabia and Jonathan Daigle

SAN DIEGO

Bassim Hamadeh, CEO and Publisher
John Remington, Executive Editor
Kaela Martin, Project Editor
Jeanine Rees, Production Editor
Jess Estrella, Senior Graphic Designer
Alexa Lucido, Licensing Supervisor
Natalie Piccotti, Director of Marketing
Kassie Graves, Vice President of Editorial
Jamie Giganti, Director of Academic Publishing

3970 Sorrento Valley Blvd., Ste. 500, San Diego, CA 92121

Table of Contents

Acknowledgments

I would like to express my gratitude to all those who supported me on this project. Especially, I would like to thank Dr. Sercan Canbolat for helping me in the process of editing and proofreading. Nobody has been more important to me in the pursuit of this book than my wife and wonderful kids. Thank you for your unending inspiration.

Hazza Abu Rabia

PART 1

Reflections on the Exiled Prophet

1

Palestinian Literature after the Nakba

HAZZA ABU RABIA

The Nakba forced most Palestinian intellectuals into exile. Most of the Palestinians who remained in Israel were peasants who lived in rural areas and lacked education. Those who had lived in cosmopolitan cities like Jaffa, Haifa, and A'kka generally were forced to flee. Israel treated all Palestinians with an iron fist and the Palestinian population lived under tight security control. For these reasons, it is not surprising that resistance literature first sprang up outside Israel's borders. Exiled poets, story writers, and intellectuals led the way, using literature of all kinds to spread awareness of the Nakba and its catastrophes and igniting the Palestinian fight against the Zionist state and its ideology. Resistance literature is "a politicized literature that actively critiques and interrogates oppressive institutions and ideologies" (Lawson 12).

The prominent Palestinian writer Ghassan Kanafani coined the term "resistance literature" (*Muqawamah*) in his 1966 study *Literature of Resistance in Occupied Palestine: 1948–1966* (Harlow 2). Kanafani's writings were instrumental in crystallizing the conviction that Palestinians, particularly of his generation, had a heartfelt duty to remain Palestinian (Kan'an 48). Simple yet profound, his work gave voice to the Palestinian longing for a free Palestine. In one of his novels, *Return to Haifa* (1969), Kanafani insists: "The greatest crime anybody can commit is to think that the weakness and the mistakes of others give him the right to exist at their expense" (35).

His *oeuvre* reflects the Palestinian memory of occupation, loss, and exile. His seminal "resistance literature" depicts Palestinians' everyday struggles. His characters do not have power, but they do have a voice (Hamdi 40). In the words of Kanafani, "[they] express their own positions without reservation" (35).

Kanafani's work helped forge a sense of national identity. Whereas most other Arabic literatures were written within the confines of their respective countries, this was not possible after the Nakba, as most Palestinian intellectuals had become refugees in other countries. Palestine was, in fact, a nationless state. As such, literature written in exile helped to strengthen Palestinian national identity by depicting a common set of experiences. Kanafani's major themes include love, family, the experience of exile, the desire to return to the homeland, the struggle of finding work, and—above all—resistance to occupying forces. Kanafani not only depicts the struggles of the Palestinian diaspora, but, by extension, the struggles of all populations affected by imperialist powers (Popular Front for the Liberation of Palestine).

One of Kanafani's best-loved novels, *Men in the Sun*, portrays the effects of the Nakba upon a group of Palestinians who are forced from their homeland. Distraught and disenchanted, several individuals follow the path of another countryman in the hopes of recovering their dignity and finding a better quality of life. In search of economic opportunity, they cross the border into Kuwait in an empty water tank. Unfortunately, the truck driver transporting them is detained by authorities, and the refugees meet their calamitous doom in the unrelenting heat of their hiding place. This novel embodies the shared experience of attempting against all odds to make a better future.

His novel, *The Land of the Sad Orange*, describes the agony of dislocation through the eyes of a child. The young protagonist is forced to grow up much too soon. He struggles to keep his family together while his father is pushed to the edge of despair by economic hardship. The story ends with a metaphor for the shrunken prospects of their sad new reality: Once the orange was ripe and full of life, now it is wrinkled and dried up. Theirs is a life devoid of hope.

Kanafani's work focuses on the struggles that those alive during the Nakba endured. But it is still relevant today, for it reflects the experience of not only the Palestinians, but of all those around the world forced to endure exile and the loss of economic stability due to political forces outside their control (Khan). His characters try desperately to maintain a sense of hope for the future. This is why his fiction remains so captivating to Palestinians and non-Palestinians alike.

Among the few Palestinian intellectuals who remained inside Israel, a different type of literature flourished; I want to call it "persistence literature." This type of literature was a result of the security measures that Israel took against any Palestinian who dared confront the new regime. Palestinians understood that Israel had come to stay, and they—the natives of the land—had become orphans who lived at the mercy of the new state. They considered it wiser to fight for equality, justice, and human rights than to fight against the existence of Israel. This strategy is clear in the writings of several intellectuals who witnessed the Nakba and did not go into exile, including Emil Habibi and, later, Naji Dhaher.

Emile Habibi, well-known politician and prolific author is best known for humorous and satirical fiction that examines the condition of Palestinians after the Nakba (Peled 185). Habibi, like his contemporaries, drew on personal experience to shed light on the new realities brought by political upheaval. His writings give insight into the condition of being a Palestinian within the confines of the newly established Israeli state (Assi 89). Whereas most other writers used allegorical accounts tinged with political activism and dissent, Habibi takes a different approach. He deploys irony and satire to illustrate the painful duality of life as a Palestinian in Israel.

In *Al-Waqā'i' al-gharībah fi 'khtifā' Sa 'īd Abī 'l-Naḥsh al-Mutashā'il*, also known as the *Pessoptimist*, Habibi represents Palestinian-Israeli realities with a pervasive irony. Certain details of his protagonist's life verge on autobiography. For example, Habibi was reluctant to leave during the Nakba. Similarly, the protagonist begins to work for the Israeli government and yet still must deal with the cognitive dissonance of perpetuating a state that is in direct conflict to his past life before the Nakba (Shihadah 7). The duality of being an Arab to the Israelis and an Israeli to those who have been exiled was a burden to Habibi and his protagonist alike. Throughout the novel, the eponymous Pessoptimist is faced with a myriad of moral dilemmas. Every move that helps the government helps subjugate the Palestinian community within the borders of Israel.

In another of his novels, *Ikhtayyi*, Habibi uses the supernatural to shed light on the conditions of Palestinian-Israelis. Instead of erasing exiled Palestinians from memory, as the Israeli state has tried to do,

Habibi brings the exiles back in an imagined present where the rules of history do not apply. Habibi makes us laugh at what one normally would consider a tragic and oppressive condition (Khater 76). He approaches the problems of Palestinian-Israeli life with comedy and this, in turn, helps us contemplate the true nature of their lives and suffering (81).

Both novels are replete with accounts of helplessness represented through satire. Also, prevalent in both accounts are the themes of loss of love and lost identity. Time and circumstance seem to dull the blow of the new-found reality, and yet as time passes, the heaviness of the political situation remains, perpetuating a sense of hopelessness that seems to have no end in sight (81).

Habibi deftly establishes a parallel between the political state and the state of those within the novel. He uses the Arabic language to af-firm Palestinian identity. He also utilizes double entendre, parables, and witty banter to capture the experience of destabilizing duality. When trained on everyday injustices, this same wit conveys both resentment and resistance. Habibi's considerable skill as a writer is evident in the seemingly effortless flow of his prose, his subtle irony, and his ability to conjure a complex reality with remarkable concision. These qualities will surely keep Habibi relevant to future readers of Arabic.

Like Habibi, Naji Dhaher writes about Palestinians inside Israel. But Dhaher, who is from the second generation of Palestinian writers and was born two years after the Nakba to a displaced family, focuses specifically on displaced Palestinians. His fiction examines the psycho-logical effects of the Nakba on the children of exiled Palestinians who live within the state of Israel. Much of his writing relates the painful but sweet memory of his family's destroyed village and the trials and suffering of his daily life inside Israel. Dhaher is a prolific writer, and his varied *oeuvre* includes love stories in addition to social criticism.

Central Themes in Dhaher's Writing

From early childhood, Dhaher saw pain and sorrow in his parents' eyes. He felt keenly his inability to comfort those he loved, so it is not sur-prising that human suffering is the primary theme of his work. Initially, critics faulted Dhaher for confining his fiction to his family's personal wound. In a phone interview with Naji Dhaher, he responded quoting the famous Arabian poet Antar ibn Shaddad who said, "Could I really run away from this wound?" Dhaher continued:

> Could anyone who saw a great incident go to sleep? How do you want me to sleep when I once had something that might have been the greatest thing in the world? What does it mean that a stranger comes from faraway lands and uproots you from your home, your land, and your country, and turns you with his strength and violence into a stranger from all that is close to your heart and soul?

It is only logical, then, that Dhaher's writing is shaped by his parents' pain and his own experience growing up in the shadow of the Nakba. His vision comes from loss and the struggle to endure loss. Accordingly, two major themes dominate his writing.

The first theme is the idea of the human being within an eternal cycle, especially adapted to Palestinian life after the Nakba. This subject is represented in many stories, most notably "The Sun Never Absent" from the short story collection *Below the Mountain,* and the story "My Father" in *The Far Horizon.* These stories deal with the death of a father and the resurrection of the son after him, meaning that as man goes away from this world, his son continues along his path and carries his heritage, which he inherited from his parents and so on. Individual human life passes, but Palestinian pain, struggle, and identity endures.

His second major theme is alienation. For example, "The Fire," from this collection, is about a young Palestinian who fell in love with an Israeli girl after moving to one of the settlements. This secret love was doomed from the start by this young man's Arab identity. When a fire breaks out in the forest near the settlement, he is immediately arrested and accused of arson, even though there is no evidence. His lover will not come forward to provide an alibi, and he chooses to accept the stranger's fate.

Taken together, the stories collected in this book represent the fate of displaced Palestinians inside their homeland, starting from the Nakba, to the period of martial law and beyond. The dream of return figures prominently in Dhaher's stories, but these stories also detail the everyday trials that Palestinians have endured and continue to endure as Israel's second-class citizens.

The Nakba Period

In "Klaris," the titular protagonist attempts to return to her youth before the Nakba. The line between her present in Nazareth and her past in the town of Haifa seems almost permeable for Klaris. Set in a single day, the story opens in the early morning as Klaris recalls a distant time and a dear companion from the Haifa of her youth. This reverie is sparked by a surprising letter that has invited Klaris to Haifa. The letter informs her that her beloved had, in fact, stayed in Haifa after the Nakba and he would love to see her and her family before he passes onward to the afterlife, for he fears that his days are limited.

Klaris, her daughter, and granddaughter embark together for Haifa. Their bus ride is a journey into the past. At this point, we see the effect of the Nakba directly upon the lives of Klaris and the rest of the Palestinians in Haifa and across Palestine. Some forty years prior, Klaris and her lover had struggled against the "Zionist gangs [that] were terrorizing the people to drive them from their city at any cost." Families fled from the Zionists. Yet Klaris remained firm in her conviction. Despite the imminent danger, Klaris would bring supplies at night to her lover among the rebels. He kept her informed of the daily progress of the revolutionary movement and shared his conviction to stay true to the cause. One fateful night, he tells Klaris that the final battle is here and that if they are successful that night the city would be theirs forever. Unfortunately, the city falls, and with this catastrophic event, a mass exodus begins. Klaris and her family are among those who flee the fallen city.

Klaris wondered what happened to her beloved and clung to hope that he survived. Time passed and Klaris married and began a family of her own. Forty years later, this letter rekindles her hope, and she would not let fate steal this moment from her. Upon arriving at Haifa, she asks her family to wait for her for a moment. She abandons her fears and runs in the direction of her beloved. She hopes to reclaim what time and circumstance have stolen from her. As she approaches his apartment, she hears screams and notices a scene near the front door. Suddenly, she realizes that she is too late. Fate has, in fact, thwarted her reunion. It was as if history had repeated itself, separating loved ones for eternity. She returns to her family bitterly disappointed, but nevertheless resilient. This story embodies the spirit of the Palestinian people. It dramatizes Palestinians' strong memory, which links their present suffering to the Nakba, but also sustains a spiritual connection to their homeland and the lost loves and lives they left behind.

"The Clever" takes this theme of pre-Nakba love story in a different direction. The protagonists fell in love in the village of their youth. Their love begins when she hears him play a song of indescribable beauty on his flute, and he realizes that he has finally discovered his muse. Their life is like a fairy tale. He plays for her every day when he returns home, and she sings the melody in greeting. Their love grows in its perfection until that fateful day in May of 1948. He returns and plays his song as usual, but his beloved does not greet him. He searches for her frantically all over town but finds only destruction and devastation. But Sirini does not give up. He travels far and wide, playing his tune, awaiting her response. One day, he finally locates her at "Masada" castle. This story is replete with allusions to the destruction that the Nakba wreaked on Palestinians. Typical of Dhaher's work, a seemingly all-encompassing destruction is met with the resilience and perseverance of family, art, and love.

It is worth noting that the Masada is a legendary Jewish stronghold where brave Jewish rebels leapt to their deaths instead of being enslaved by the invading Romans in the first Jewish-Roman War. Dhaher appropriates the Masada as a legendary site of human resistance to oppression. In naming the castle where his Palestinian protagonist finds and liberates his lover from the "Masada," Dhaher suggests that the roles of oppressor and victim are contingent and shifting.

"Klaris" and "The Clever" embody the spirit of the times of the Nakba. They recall the peaceful lives that Palestinians had enjoyed pre-Nakba. Each focuses on an idyllic romance to relate the damage that the Nakba brought to individual lives. Both stories show how families and lovers were separated by the circumstances of this invasion. Most importantly, though, the stories evince love's persistence in the face of oppression. Though separated, the lovers endure hardships and trudge through history in search of an ultimate reunion. Unfortunately, not all those afflicted by the Nakba could experience the quintessential fairy tale reunion.

The Martial Law Period

Dhaher's "A Few Hours in Heaven" focuses on a family's struggles in the years after the Nakba. The mother worked wherever she could to support her household. Despite their efforts, the other members of the household were unable to find work, and the family scraped out a meager life. Dhaher captures the everyday challenges and sorrows of life at the socioeconomic margins. The family's lands have been commandeered, and they face constant discrimination. After dinner one evening, the mother informs the family that she has lost her job, and the father and the uncle must search for work with redoubled desperation. The men look like "strange thin ghosts, walking on the rough land of Nazareth." This simple description suggests the struggle of Palestinians in Israel in the time of martial law. Although the protagonists' bodies are weakened, they persevere out of love for their family. The young child, who narrates the story, comes up with an ingenious plan to earn money. He approaches a wealthy landowner and proposes that they work in his garden for an honest wage. The landowner agrees, and they begin to work diligently. After working so hard they take a moment to rest and begin to eat fruit from the trees in the garden. They also pick some to take home. As they are walking away from the job, the landowner furiously attacks them and curses them and their ancestors. They have "taken" the best fruit from the garden. The landowner had not heeded his maid's warning against hiring refugees. The father, uncle, and son were merely trying to survive. Yet the landowner could not see their struggle. He saw only a group of ragged refugees who "ruined" his garden.

In "The Hyena of Sartaba," Dhaher tells of a struggling family in similar straits. A Palestinian father in a family of Sirini refugees had been working with a Jewish employer for a period of years in the town of Haifa. When the father loses his job, the father, uncle and son resort to desperate measures to keep the family afloat. They undertake a perilous quest. Dhaher mixes the mythical and mundane expertly. To keep the family alive, the three set out for the forest to harvest licorice root, the crucial ingredient in a drink they intend to bottle and sell to workers. But this forest is the home of the fearsome ghoul of Sartaba. Again, here we see an important allusion: Sartaba was known as a fortress used to house political prisoners (Rocca). The father, uncle, and son dress in British military attire and set off on their quest. This too was indicative of the times. Young children had to grow up fast; they contributed to the well-being of the family in any way that they could. The three enter the forest in the thick of the night and work hastily. Before they have harvested enough licorice root, they are confronted by the ghoul, a monstrous hyena. The father realizes that to save his family, he must sacrifice himself. He strips naked and approaches the hyena, leaving the uncle and asking him to take care of his family for him. The father tries reasoning with the hyena as the other two continue to work. The father's effort is in vain, however. And the hyena is not satisfied with one victim. The ghoul returns to prey on the uncle and son. The uncle understands that he must also sacrifice himself to ensure the safety of the son and the rest of the family. He reminds his nephew to "live and carry our message." The uncle approaches the hyena and meets his fate. The son is spared by the sacrifices of the older generation and obtains the necessary licorice root. The ending is bittersweet. The boy understands that his life has been saved at the expense of the lives of his father and uncle. But he also feels a new responsibility for the future of the family.

"The Departure" also dramatizes the hardships of the post-Nakba years. The title has a double meaning, not only referencing loved ones that have departed from this earthly plane, but also those who "departed" from their homeland after the Nakba. When the patriarch dies, his family attempts to bury him in a cemetery in Nazareth. They are turned away and told that he must be buried in the strangers' cemetery. The patriarch had always wanted to return to his homeland of Sirin. He had told his son how the family came to be in their present situation and how he had toiled for years in Haifa for a Jewish employer, doing very hard work for little pay. He had lived a difficult life, taking very little for himself and sacrificing all that he had for his family. He told his children of the lands they once owned and shared fond memories of Sirin. After the Nakba, he and his family were forbidden from returning to their lands. Under martial law, the land where his destroyed village once stood was considered a "military zone." Upon returning to their old lands after martial law was finally lifted, the family experienced the extremes of joy and sorrow. The story ends by bearing witness to the sad reality of exile: The father's dying wish cannot be fulfilled, and he is buried in a strange land. His funeral is poorly attended, and the family is forced to find comfort in themselves. But this is not the end. The father remains a "restive witness" of what occurred during the Nakba. His family maintains the memory of the past.

The Dream of Return (Keeping the Memory of the Nakba Alive for New Generations)

"Meow of the Mountain" is a curious tale of a man who visits his sister after a long separation. En route, he recalls the events that have led to this moment: his life after the Nakba, his disapproval of his sister's marriage, their gradual drifting apart, and his lifetime of working tirelessly to one day buy a house and reclaim some of the dignity he lost with his old home in his destroyed village. Now past middle age, he is on the brink of despair, having had his life's savings stolen. He realizes it would take another lifetime to recoup his loss, and just as his thoughts turn their darkest, he crosses paths with a cat. He wonders if the cat, too, was also displaced due to the events of the Nakba. He searches frantically for the cat, but to no avail. He then remembers his purpose and heads to his sister's home. He walks and then runs toward this reunion. Perhaps he would be fortunate enough to find the mysterious cat there.

"Displaced, Son of a Displaced" is thematically similar. In this tale, the protagonist recalls his former life. He remembers the effect of the Nakba upon himself and his family, which has recently been further fractured. His daughter was kicked out of her household, and his immediate goal is to bring her back into the fold. Again, Dhaher builds toward an ending that affirms life, family, and memory, as the protagonist runs through the night without assurance of the future but with hope.

Finally, in "Woman of Love," a man writes a letter to a former lover. He recounts their early life together and reminds her of what he had done to impress her when he was a leader in their village of Sirin before the Nakba. He also recounts his love for her and for the place he once called home. These memories live within him, and he will not forget his lover or his village. He insists that what they still share outweighs their differences, and he implores her to return to resurrect the lost city's soul and to resurrect love.

Discrimination against Palestinians in Israel

Discrimination is a prominent theme in the volume's final four stories, set closer to the present. "Accused on the Beach" unfolds as a conversation between the protagonist and the authorities, who have cited him for fishing illegally. The accused is a displaced Palestinian, who was not fully aware of the restriction on fishing in Lake Tiberias. He claims ignorance and explains that he had never even held a balbout fish before. When a stranger presented this fish to him, he was naturally perplexed, so he asked his estranged wife for advice, which led him to return the fish to its waters. But when he returned to the lake, he did not heed the sign indicating that he was forbidden from entering the beach. Authorities, therefore, charged him with the crimes of entering a prohibited area and fishing illegally. After his long, often humorous explanation, the judge nevertheless finds him guilty. Dhaher's representation of anti-Arab discrimination combines the fabulous and the mundane, as the accused becomes a kind of Palestinian everyman caught in a system he does not fully understand.

In "The Fire," Dhaher approaches discrimination from another angle. A young Palestinian is with his Israeli lover when a fire breaks out near their settlement. A newcomer, he is also the settlement's only Arab. The lovers face a terrible dilemma: She could give him an alibi, but this would expose their illicit romance. He considers running away, but this would tear him from his lover and make him seem even guiltier. Realizing that as an Arab he was guilty until proven innocent and that proving his innocence would come at too high of a cost, he decides to confess to arson and is forced to recreate his supposed crime for the authorities. The story ends with a newspaper headline that an Arab was committing arson for the second time when he was confronted and shot.

In the "Land of Terror," a Palestinian grandfather takes a break from his writing to spend time with his granddaughter near a local mall. The two enjoy each other's company, but the young girl soon grows tired and asks for her parents. When they return to the mall, they find the entrance blocked off and armed guards milling about. The grandfather tries reasoning with the guard, who responds unsympathetically. This scene suggests that no Arabs are above suspicion, neither young nor old. At a loss, the grandfather remembers a hole in the perimeter wall.

He walks his granddaughter to it and furtively helps her through the opening so she can find her parents. As he tries to follow her through, a guard stops him. His thoughts race: Would she be reunited with her parents? Such is the life of Palestinians. Suddenly, his pleasant day is gone, and reality closes in on the writer. Everything inside of him wants to implore the guards to allow him to be reunited with his family. But he is paralyzed with fear as the soldiers surround him.

Featuring another writer-protagonist, "A Very Ordinary Scene" dramatizes a commonplace occurrence. A journalist is returning home from a long day at work. He recalls his wife's repeated warnings about driving too fast and his response that Arab drivers are often pulled over for little or no reason. As he crosses an intersection, he nearly collides with another car, but his luck holds up. Moments later, however, he notices a police car coming up from behind. He pulls aside to allow the officer to pass, but the officer stops him instead. Other police cars arrive suddenly. An officer asks for his documentation and accuses him of a traffic infraction. Although he disagrees, there is nothing the protagonist can do. The near accident was not his fault, and the encounter humiliates him. When he finally makes it home and recounts the traffic stop to his wife, the tension breaks for a moment. They joke about future incidents, and she threatens to call the police on him if he ever speeds. But this playfulness is an act on his part. The journalist retreats to his room. Tears well in his eyes but do not fall. He is frustrated by the injustice of his situation, but such is his reality. It is an everyday burden that he must bear.

Works Cited

Assi, Seraje. "Memory, Myth and the Military Government: Emile Habibi's Collective Autobiography." *Jerusalem Quarterly* 52, 2013, p. 89.

Hamdi, Tahrir. "Bearing witness in Palestinian resistance literature". *SAGE Journal*. Vol 52, Issue 3, 2011, https://doi.org/10.1177/0306396810390158.

Harlow, Barbara. *Resistance Literature*. Routledge, 1987.

Kanafani, Ghassan. *The 1936-39 Revolt in Palestine*. Committee for a Democratic Palestine, 1972, New York.

——. *'Ā'id ilá Ḥayfā*. Remal Publication, 2015.

Khan Mohsin. "Ghassan Kanafani. Ra'id Dirasat al-Adab al-Muwawim wa al-Adab a-Sahiouni." *Aljazeera*. Jul 22, 2018, https://blogs.aljazeera.net/blogs/2018/7/22/. Accessed March 2019.

Khater, Akram. "Emile Habibi: The Mirror of Irony in Palestinian Literature". *Journal of Arabic Literature*, Vol. 24, No. 1, 1993, p 76.

Lawson, Marie. *Resistance and Resilience in the Work of Four Native American Authors*. 2016. University of Arizona, PhD dissertation, p. 12. http://hdl.handle.net/10150/193773.

Peled, Assaf. "Descending the Khazooq: Working through, the Trauma of the Nakba in Emile Habibi's Oeuvre". *Israel Studies*, 2016, Vol. 21(1), pp. 157–182.

Popular Front for the Liberation of Palestine. "Comrade Ghassan Kanafani: The leader, the writer, the Martyr". 2012 http://pflp.ps/english/2012/07/08/comrade-ghassan-kanafani-the-leader-the-writer-the-martyr/.Accessed 10 March 2019.

Rocca, Samuel. *The Forts of Judaea 168 BC-AD 73*. 2008, Osprey Publishing. Oxford, United Kingdom.

Shihadah, Sarah, *Buried: The Defiant Unspoken in Emile Habiby's The Pessoptimist*. University of Pennsylvania, Undergraduate Humanities Forum 2013–2014: Violence, 2. https://repository.upenn.edu/uhf_2014/2/. Accessed 10 March 2019.

Kan'an 48. "Ghassan-Kanafani Political-Writings". *WordPress, Palestine Diary Blog*.29 November 2015, https://kanan48.wordpress.com/ghassan-kanafani/political-writings/. Accessed 10 March 2019.

2

Naji Dhaher and Internal Exile

JONATHAN DAIGLE

I. Internal Exile and Palestinian-Israeli Experience

Although Naji Dhaher was born in present-day Nazareth Illit in 1951, in his fiction he returns time and again to his family's village of Sirin, destroyed in 1948. Dhaher was born into a uniquely Palestinian condition of internal exile. The collected stories and novella in *The Exiled Prophet* express this condition in different registers. Dhaher's perspective on internal exile is not unique for a Palestinian-Israeli, but it is unique for a Palestinian writer. As Hazza Abu Rabia notes in the previous chapter, most Palestinian writers and intellectuals living in what became Israel in 1948 went into exile, either by choice or by force, after the Nakba. One exception is the beloved Mahmoud Darwish, who is widely regarded as the poet laureate of Palestine. Darwish was six years old when his family's village was seized and eventually razed by occupying forces. His experience as an "internal refugee" or "present-absent alien" inspired poems such as his famous "Identity Card." But even Darwish would eventually leave. He had been in exile for years when he wrote "I Belong There" with its haunting final line: "I have learned and dismantled all the words in order to draw from them a single word: *Home*" (7). Darwish epitomizes the double loss shared by many Palestinian writers. Not only did he lose the village of his ancestors when his family was forced from Birwe, but he was also exiled from Israel in 1970 and compelled to seek home in what he called "the deep horizon of my word" (7).

Dhaher writes from a similar yet different place. As an internal exile from the moment of his birth in an abandoned British military building atop a mountain overlooking Nazareth, Dhaher has always lived tantalizingly close to his family's lost village of Sirin. Because internal exile is arguably the unifying theme of both this volume and Palestinian-Israel experience, it will be useful to define the concept, starting with the condition of exile more broadly. No Palestinian writer has contributed more to our understanding of this condition than Edward Said. In "Reflections on Exile," Said describes exile as "the unhealable rift forced between a human being and a native place, between the self and its true home: its essential sadness can never be surmounted" (173). Said is careful not to romanticize this "condition of terminal loss" (173). Nevertheless, he argues that because "exiles are aware of at least two [cultures, they possess a] plurality of vision [that] gives rise to an awareness of simultaneous dimensions, an awareness that—to borrow a phrase from music—is *contrapuntal*" (186). While the experience of homelessness often drives suffering individuals toward nationalism, exiles may also derive painful insight from their border-crossing, barrier-breaking experiences (186). Exiles' contrapuntal experience may help them see beyond nationalism, dogma and narrow ideas of home (186). Such a perspective on orthodoxy and prejudice is the hallmark of Said's work. But this contrapuntal perspective is not available, as such, to internal exiles such as Dhaher, who live in a country built on the erasure of their identity and homeland. Palestinian-Israelis experience multiple cultures, but not in a way that is likely to produce a "plurality of vision" (186).

To contextualize Dhaher's representation of the unique Palestinian-Israeli condition of exile, I would first like to illustrate the experience of Sayed Kashua, the ground-breaking Palestinian-Israeli writer and humorist. Kashua was raised in the Palestinian town of Tira but attended Israel's most prestigious Hebrew-language school as one of very few Arab students. He developed his voice as a columnist in a left-leaning Hebrew-language newspaper, *Haaretz*, where he still regularly contributes. Kashua was already an acclaimed novelist and memoirist when he achieved a stunning breakthrough in 2007 with *Arab Labor*, the first predominantly Arab-language program on Israel's Channel 2. He and his wife settled as the only Arab family in a Jewish neighborhood in Jerusalem, and his children eventually attended the area's only bilingual school.

No other Arab writer had made such inroads into Israeli intellectual and popular culture, but even Kashua found his situation untenable during the violent summer of 2014. Kashua had secured a visiting professor position at the University of Illinois and he and his family intended to return home after his term was through. As conditions worsened, however, they decided to move up their departure date and extend their stay in the United States indefinitely. In his farewell column, "Why Sayed Kashua Is Leaving Jerusalem and Never Coming Back," he expressed concern for his family's safety and asked: "What is there for me in Israel?" Israel's drift further toward Jewish nationalism in recent years has only confirmed the sad necessity of his exile. After the 2018 Nationality Law, which solidified Arab Israelis' second-class status, Kashua wrote an editorial in the *New York Times* describing his efforts at explaining Israeli apartheid to his children:

> It seeks to legislate what Israel has been effectively telling non-Jewish minorities all along: You will never be a part of this country, you will never be equal, you are doomed to be unwanted citizens forever, to be inferior to the Jews to whom the state belongs and for whom it was founded. A state in which Judaism is the only national expression permissible by law will, by definition, reject any minority member who wishes to be part of it, even if he is, like me, fluent in its culture or, as I do, writes literature in its language, respects its laws, serves its society.

This turn of events weighed heavily on Kashua, who had dedicated his career to bringing the Arab and Jewish worlds of Israel together. Indeed, nearly all of his varied creative work argues for the necessity of dissolving stereotypes and other barriers of hate and ignorance. He aimed to promote understanding and walked the walk in his education and everyday life. Yet even his rare inter-cultural experience ended in exile. There is perhaps wisdom in such exile, as Kashua's recent work suggests, but also irrevocable loss. To protect their children and their futures, he and his wife were forced to endure a painful separation from their own families and from the history, living conditions, and culture that made them who they are. In a 2014 column in *Haaretz*, Kashua describes feeling compelled by a sense of loss and homesickness to zoom in on his parents' home in Google Earth, as if the internet could close the distance (Margalit 18). Family is the foundation of Palestinian-Israeli identity, and as Kashua's experience demonstrates, exile can strain inter-generational bonds. Kashua's parents' loss is not identical to his loss, and his children have become acculturated to their new home. Kashua acknowledges the divergence between his children's reality and his own in the *New York Times* editorial, cited above. After hearing of the privileges accorded Jewish Israelis by the Nationality Law, his youngest child asks, "Can't we be Jewish, then?"

II. Exile and Inheritance in Dhaher's Short Stories

Even before he left Israel, exile's contrapuntal perspective was difficult for Kashua to sustain. Seeing the Arab-Jewish conflict from two perspectives meant giving equal weight to a point of view determined to erase his identity and family history. When this became undeniably clear and when this hostility impinged on his family's life, exile abroad was the obvious choice. The contrapuntal perspective Said describes is still not viable for Dhaher, who writes in Arabic and lives and works like most Palestinian-Israelis within Israel's Arab community.

For Dhaher, identity and family are co-extensive ideas, and each is rooted in the living memory of the Nakba. That is, his perspective is rooted in conflict, albeit a conflict he did not choose. Dhaher's protagonists often confront the reality that what they have lost will not be recovered in their lifetimes. This realization raises the specter of despair, and it places great pressure on the next generation. For this reason, the prospect of Palestine's lost villages becoming lost to memory carries special poignancy in his work. Dhaher is not unfamiliar with Western culture or literature. In fact, a deep knowledge of other literatures and traditions enriches his work. One cannot read *The Exiled Prophet* without thinking of Gogol, Joyce, and Kafka. My point is that by condition and choice, Dhaher holds a more conservative attitude toward Palestinian culture, rooted ultimately in a sense of what has been lost and how it was lost. While it is true that exile is always about loss, Dhaher dramatizes the unique orientation toward loss of the internal exile. Again, to acknowledge the legitimacy of the Israeli perspective would be to adopt a point of view that is hostile to your existence, as

Kashua ultimately conceded. Further, internal exile is not an exile in the usual sense of geographic and cultural separation from the place where one was raised and called home. This is especially true for Palestine's second-generation internal exiles. For Dhaher, home is a pale version of the lost village, but it nonetheless roots him in his culture and its history and offers an experience of family and community.

In *The Exiled Prophet*, Dhaher's responses to displacement and internal exile range from fantasies of recovery, including "The Clever" and "Women of Love," to expressions of apartheid fatigue such as "The Fire," "The Land of Terror," and "A Very Ordinary Scene." These extremes have more in common than at first appears. Dhaher's stories of recovered wholeness incorporate elements of magical realism. They describe villages that rise out of rubble and lovers and artists who repel invasions through art and imagination. Such stories contain a dream-like quality, but they should not be dismissed as wishful fantasies. The volume's last short stories, however, permit no magical solution to the experience of internal exile. In journalistic realism, Dhaher documents the pressure of daily inhumanities. The lover of "The Fire" realizes it is futile to protest a false accusation and complies with his abusive accusers, becoming Israeli newspapers' bad Arab *de jure*, and the protagonists in "Land of Terror" and "A Very Ordinary Scene" are both paralyzed by feelings of powerlessness. In the former, the writer-protagonist opens his mouth but cannot speak to soldiers who stand between himself and his family. In the latter, the writer-protagonist retreats to the sanctuary of his room after being harassed by the police; his eyes tear but he cannot cry.

Although they seem antithetical, fantasy and frustration are mutually constitutive responses to the internal exile's psychological experience. The magical reversals of political history that Dhaher describes in "The Clever" and "Woman of Love" reflect the absurdity of living in one's own land as a foreigner, enemy, or pseudo-citizen. It makes sense then to read Dhaher's fantasies of recovery and accounts of frustration as two reactions to the same problem of loss, set in motion by the upheaval of 1948 and central to Palestinian-Israeli identity and experience today. In Dhaher's fantasy, love and art reverse time and reinstate Arab humanity. In his somber realism, lovers and artists who commemorate this humanity in word and deed are ultimately silenced by their oppressors.

Yet Palestinian-Israeli humanity, the unifying testimony of Dhaher's *oeuvre*, is just as clearly dramatized in its denial as in its imaginative triumphs. Indeed, the humanity of Dhaher's suffering protagonists is made visible by their counterparts' refusal to see it. Further, this suffering assumes meaning in service to the dream of return, if not to lost Sirin, then to freedom and humanity.

When Kashua found it impossible to believe that Israel would ever grant Arabs such humanity, he chose exile. The stories in this volume emerge from the pressure of internal exile. They work through different responses to the same troubling realization. Despair, necessity, and implacable agents of the state stalk Dhaher's protagonists in different forms and combinations across these twelve narratives. Recovery and paralysis, imaginative fantasy, and documentary realism bookend a broad continuum of responses to this beset state. Most of these stories fall in between. Characters wrestle with internal exile and find some meaning in their struggle to sustain family, culture, and identity, even though each is paradoxically rooted in displacement. Often, this meaning comes from reconnecting with estranged family members or lost lovers. Nearly as often this search for meaning is less a product of reasoned reflection than it is a leap of faith. In "Klaris," "The Meow of the Mountain," and "Displaced, Son of a Displaced," for example, protagonists literally run through the streets toward an uncertain reunion with what they have lost.

In Dhaher's world, Palestinian life and loss are mutually constitutive; the lost village is always literally a lost village, an unrecoverable world, but the shared memory of loss nevertheless preserves a living identity. This identity is often portrayed by Dhaher in aesthetic or spiritual terms, as in the flute music of "The Clever" through which the lost village is reformed and defended from repeated invasion. More often in these short stories, characters must struggle to preserve whatever family they have, and this struggle sustains a shared culture and identity. Several of these stories dramatize the passing of responsibility for family and culture from father to son. For instance, the first-person narrator of "The Departure" is a son who has inherited his father's exile as a debt he cannot pay. In a startling dream sequence, the father stabs his son in the back and asks: "Will I be buried in this beloved land or in a strange place?" With no choice, the son ultimately buries his father in the strangers' cemetery, and his father's soul cannot find peace. The dream of return is vividly represented in "A Few Hours in Heaven." Amid his family's struggle to survive, the young narrator describes how he would "[take] refuge in distant gardens dreamt of by my family but never touched by their exiled feet." The loss and the compensating dream have been passed down through the generations. In this coming-of-age story, the boy takes responsibility for his impoverished family's welfare by leading his father and uncle to a garden in a wealthy Jewish neighborhood where they can work for pay. The story ends abruptly, when, after an idyllic afternoon, the three workers are driven from the garden. Dhaher appropriates the Old Testament creation story to allegorize Israel's founding appropriation of Palestine, his lost Eden, but something else is going on here. The young first-person narrator has inherited his family's dream, its loss, and its livelihood of struggle. His experience of the garden and its loss affirm his family heritage of exile, memory, and solidarity. He found the garden for himself and he has experienced its loss, growing from innocence to knowledge. The story is an allegory of the Nakba, its terror and loss, but it also dramatizes the inheritance of loss as the ground of Palestinian identity. When the young boy leaves the garden, he takes his memory of the garden with him. "The Hyena of Sartaba" is even more explicit in rooting the meaning and fullness of Palestinian life in an orientation toward loss. Again, a young boy joins his father and uncle in a desperate plan to support his family. Crushing poverty leads them to Sartaba, home to a mythical predator. The father and the uncle sacrifice themselves for the son, who leaves the forest in the morning aware that "a new life was conferred on me by my father and my uncle." He journeys home through the dawn with a harvest of licorice root and "the feeling that I had just suffered a terrible loss and had received my life back at the same time." The protagonist emerges with the roots his family needs to survive, suggesting, of course, that the rootedness lost in exile can be found in family and family history. Family is the vessel that carries culture and identity through the vulnerability and humiliation of internal exile.

III. Forms of Exile in *The Owl Neighborhood*

In a remarkable blend of humor, pathos, melodrama, and the picaresque, *The Owl Neighborhood* examines internal exile from multiple angles. The novella is not a tragedy by any means, but it has roots in the Nakba. Its protagonist, Raqraq al-Sharif, is a plucky *picaro* in the tradition of Don Quixote. He has left the afterlife in hopes of reuniting with the fractured family that he left years earlier. The implication is that exile from his family has made eternal rest impossible for Raqraq, even though his memories of the afterlife suggest he was popular and contented there. Raqraq is a comic version of the restive father of "The Departure," who cannot find peace in the strangers' cemetery and haunts a foreign land. For Dhaher, family has the power to affirm a common past and thereby shelter Palestinian identity from hostile forces bent on effacing it. Family is a powerful mode of belonging and, as such, the ground for full personhood. In *The Owl Neighborhood* family does not simply protect against exile. It is an imperfect yet necessary sanctuary and is rooted in the experience of exile. For Raqraq, family is the flower of exile. He does not return to transcend or overcome exile. He returns to make it livable. By sharing his experience of loss with his family, he turns loss into a condition of belonging.

In Raqraq's opening soliloquy, which spans the entire first chapter, Dhaher signals a complex, mutually informing relationship between loss and identity, exile and family. In the very first paragraph, Raqraq identifies himself as one of "the sons of the Palestinian family whose fathers were expelled from their homeland." Raqraq was also exiled from his family by divorce and is a stranger in the new neighborhood where his ex-wife, Zeina al-Sha'sha'a, has resettled. She is now married to a violent yob, the aptly named Sama'an al-Atrash. Raqraq understands his quest as an effort to bring his former wife back into the fold of Palestinian culture. He tells his loyal son and plotting partner, Husam: "[Your mother], like us, lives in a forced exile. The West deceived her with its laws. But I am confident that the smell of the land of our village, Sirin, will return her to her roots." Raqraq's phrasing is interesting here. He does not expect that Zeina will literally visit Sirin, Baysan, which was destroyed in 1948. Instead, he imagines himself as an embodiment of the lost presence of their village. He *is* Zeina's connection to Sirin, and vice versa. His plan to win her back depends on Zeina's sharing his conception of exile, its value, and its centrality to her identity. He hopes to restore himself, his wife, and his family to the old ways predicated on a shared regard for what has been lost. Zeina does not value exile in the same way he does, however, even though she seeks a better life for their children. During their marriage, Raqraq unwittingly alienated Zeina when he spent his time "devilling in the wilderness of stories, hoping to write one that could lift [the family] upward." When the new women's protection law made it easier for women to file for divorce, Zeina jumped at the chance. Raqraq views this same law as an unwelcome western import. For Zeina, however, western culture and its liberal gender laws offer a path out of the second-class citizenship that Palestinian-Israelis face. After settling her divorce, she uses Lebanese mega-star Haifa Wehbe as a model for her daughters' potential careers. Each parent seeks relief from poverty and second-class status through the arts. Raqraq's writing is consistent with the old ways, while Zeina's pop star ambition is decidedly western.

The uncertain journey through exile to full personhood is the unifying theme of this volume. What is so fascinating about *The Owl Neighborhood* is that it sets competing ideas of full personhood against one another. Raqraq stakes his and his family's restored humanity to the restoration of the old patriarchy. The novel is essentially a quixotic quest to redo the past. Raqraq must have known that this was a longshot, given his comic assessment of his marriage as a war that ended only when he finally left the house waving a white flag. It was not a peaceful union. Upon his return, after several years away and a brief stint in the afterlife, Raqraq is directed by his son to the new family home, where he watches his ex-wife through the kitchen window and quips: "Look! She is still holding a knife and cutting things. Damn you, woman! You must have cut a great many things in your life! No one in this world has suffered from your practice of cutting more than me." He proves prophetic, too, as moments later, Zeina cuts his hands, sending him tumbling from her third-floor window. This association with knives and cutting things suggests that Zeina has long claimed the authority that Raqraq feels should be reserved for men. There is little question that Dhaher's sympathies are with the displaced father and the things he values: the written word, family, cultural continuity, and the Palestine he has lost but has not given up on. Zeina, however, is more than a melodramatic villain. That role is instead reserved for her abusive new husband. Zeina's energy and ambition steal the show on several occasions. While it would take some imagination to see her as the text's hero, she does send Rarqraq, the uninvited, inconvenient revenant falling from his voyeur's perch and the detestable Sama'an sprawling to a violent death. She is no pushover and she knows what she wants. She comes across less as a hateful embodiment of western values, and more as the heroine of a 1930s screwball comedy or a Shakespearean romance. She and her ex-husband simply respond to exile and marginalization in different ways.

The novel as a form developed out of the increasing uncertainty of the individual's relationship to society in the modern world with its accelerated patterns of change, shifting values, and destabilized hierarchies. Dhaher uses the form to flesh out multiple, competing perspectives on Palestinian-Israeli experience. Specifically, the conflict between Raqraq and Zeina suggests that gender may moderate one's views on internal exile. Zeina may appear greedy or domineering in her pursuit of fame and wealth, but her longing for control over her own life is understandable. More importantly, even though the novel seems to represent the women's protection law as antithetical to Palestinian values and traditions, it makes sense that Zeina would identify the law with new possibilities, even new freedoms, which is to say that the experience of exile in *The Owl Neighborhood* is valued differently by its principal male and female characters. For Raqraq, the path to full personhood must run through the past. But for Zeina, the past represents not only the dislocation of the Nakba, but also the disfranchisement of patriarchy. There is very little violence in this collection, so the two major instances of violence perpetrated by Arab characters are instructive, for they point in different directions. In a dream sequence in "The Departure," a father stabs his son for failing to bury his body in his home village. Conversely, Zeina kills her domineering second husband for blocking her path to an imagined future. She does this after stabbing her first husband, who identifies himself with their lost village of Sirin. Clearly, this is a couple with irreconcilable views on the past and the future. Zeina resorts to violence to open an alternative future, for she has become disenchanted with the things that are most important to Raqraq. He knows this, but he perseveres out of a desperate need to share his experience of exile. He cannot accept that the things he has valued could die with him.

Raqraq rises from his grave to reunite his family and overcome his lonely fate—a mirror image of the plight of the father in "The Hyena of Sartaba," who must die to sustain his family and his connection to a beloved past. To restore the meaning of the past and, therefore, the meaning of his own life, Raqraq must return to life. Back in the world of the living, however, Raqraq quickly finds that he has no home. Raqraq's home base in *The Owl Neighborhood* is neither the apartment up the red stairs, where his wife and her new husband live, nor the home of his twin daughters and their twin husbands, where he is a welcome outsider. It is the forest, a place of fear and darkness, which recalls "the perilous territory of not-belonging," the world "beyond the frontier of 'us' and the 'outsiders'" in Edward Said's conception of exile (177). Raqraq, in fact, resembles one of the two voices in Darwish's beautiful memorial poem, "Counterpoint: Homage to Edward Said." This voice asserts: "I shall construct myself and choose my exile."

Raqraq's quest teeters on the edge between the exile he fears and the exile he longs for, between the lost connection of "non-belonging" and the shared experience of loss, which becomes the ground for a viable, if imperfect, identity. His problem is that he cannot simply choose his own exile. Ostensibly, he tried that in the intervening years between his divorce and his death. Whatever stories he produced in these unaccounted years were not enough for him to rest in peace. Again, for Raqraq, family is the flower of exile. After learning that he cannot rest without restoring his connection to his family, which is his connection to both the past and future, he attempts to turn back time. In this way, Raqraq is like Jay Gatsby, who responds to narrator Nick Carraway's warning, "You can't repeat the past," quite innocently with "Why of course you can!" (Fitzgerald 110). To repeat the past, Raqraq needs to convince his wife that the past is worth the effort. Making peace with his wife would turn back time and restore Raqraq's experience of a "state of belonging" that is defined by trauma and loss. He is not trying to recover an idealized or unbroken past, but the recent past that he and his family created against the dehumanizing experience of internal exile. He learns that even this past cannot be recovered because his wife does not value it the way he does. Because the smell of Sirin does not move her, he is reduced to the forest.

The novella ends with an unplanned rendezvous of the text's surviving male characters: Raqraq, Husam, and his erstwhile sons-in-law. (Also present is Raqraq's mystical owl, gendered female, perhaps in a kind of wish fulfilment—more on this owl in a moment.) The twin sons-in-law have come to share their common defeat; their wives, Raqraq's twin daughters, have left to follow their mother's pop star dreams. With nothing else to do, they come to hear the story Raqraq had promised to tell them. This is appropriate. Widely loved by his fellow dead in the afterlife, Raqraq's stories are a bridge to what has been lost. Raqraq, however, does not recite one of his stories. Instead, he delivers a lecture on their shared predicament. He focuses on the fundamental cultural differences between Arab and Jewish culture. He connects his personal quest to reunite his family to the Palestinian quest for freedom, and he conditions this freedom on a return to patriarchy. The novella opens with Raqraq implicitly comparing his family's exile at the hands of Israel to the struggle with Zeina that led to his divorce. The novella's core political and romantic conflicts are aligned once again in this final chapter.

It seems clear that Dhaher speaks through Raqraq on some level and shares his protagonist's criticism of western values, including topsy-turvy gender relations, gross sensuality, and crass materialism. But Dhaher also recognizes that these judgments stem from a certain point of view. Indeed, Raqraq focuses on cultural differences—not absolute ones. He tells the gathered men: "[W]e live in a time of transition, and someone has to pay the price. I do not believe that any Arab house will be spared these changes. The pain of transformation will enter our houses one by one, and it will drive a wedge between many husbands and their wives, and it will alienate many children from their parents." His immediate concern is that "the laws, which are implemented in this country, regarding our home life, especially the women's protection law, are products of Europe. These laws are good for Europe, but they do not fit our culture." Notice who identifies with Arab culture and where they are: Four men who, having been routed and forced to retreat, have assembled in the darkness of the forest to lick their wounds and plan their next step. They are paying the price. The women in the novella see change in a different way. They do not see a retrenchment of the old ways as the best response to the Palestinian condition of second-class citizenship.

Instead of resolving this intra-cultural tension, Dhaher shifts his narrative to a different register in this final scene. The novella's main concern is not with modernity's effects on Palestinian-Israeli identity but on how individuals preserve their identities in the face of such forces. In an ending that suggests the Christian story of Christ's ascension to heaven forty days after his resurrection from death, Raqraq ends his quest where it began, in the afterlife. His son's love has prepared Raqraq to move on. By following his mysterious owl out of the painful experience of exile within exile, Raqraq transcends a condition that Said describes as "like death but without death's ultimate mercy" (174). In Raqraq's guardian owl, Dhaher folds together Arab associations of owls with death, western notions of owls and wisdom, and perhaps the Christian Holy Spirit, often figured as a bird. The owl is a spiritual presence throughout Raqraq's journey; in times of need, it inspires and revives both father and son. Further, the Holy Spirit, often represented as a dove, is closely associated with the Resurrection and Ascension stories of the New Testament. This is germane to Raqraq's journey, which begins in a resurrection and ends, when Raqraq proclaims: "I must return to the other world ... where my friends await me." The owl, like the Holy Spirit, is "the link that connects the worlds," as Raqraq tells his son and sons-in-law. We know that Dhaher incorporates biblical allusions in his fiction, so it is not too much of a stretch to see Raqraq in the forest with his son and sons-in-law as a version of Jesus with his disciples before he ascends into heaven.

Raqraq's final walk into the darkness may represent a kind of victory over death. Raqraq follows the owl back to the comforts of the next life, and "in the final moment before [his father] disappeared forever, Husam ran after him to say one last thing, but the darkness swallowed Raqraq before the son could speak." The narrator asks: "Were those words: 'I promise, my father, to preserve everything beautiful you left behind?'" And concludes: "Maybe ... Perhaps ... Who knows?" We never find out what Husam would have said, but the narrator's speculation rings true, for Husam has demonstrated his love throughout his father's doomed quest. In fact, Husam's love makes Raqraq's quest a success on one important level. If one accepts what seems implicit in the final paragraph, that Husam is prepared to carry the torch of the old ways and the old loss into the future, it follows that Raqraq has passed on an important part of himself, his family, and his culture. Husam's reward for filial loyalty is the experience of beauty and a living connection to the past. Moreover, the unspoken promise of preserving everything beautiful that his father has left behind positions Husam to make distinctions. He can choose his inheritance, which means he can grow. He can decide what is beautiful. He can carry what he loves of the past into the future, protecting it from oblivion so that the Nakba is not a full erasure of Palestinian identity. After all, Raqraq's quest was always about keeping cultural memory alive.

Raqraq returned so that he might share his struggle with this family. He could not rest knowing that the past he valued might be coextensive with his own life. In other words, he could not accept an idea of exile as "terminal loss" (Said 173). By the end of his journey, he has not overcome the condition of internal exile, but he has managed to share the best parts of his experience with his loving son. In a sense, he has chosen his own exile, but, more importantly, he has shared it. Like Jesus in the Christian story of the Ascension, Raqraq returns to the other world, but leaves behind a gift. His gift is not the Holy Spirit, as such, but the experience of beauty and the agency to select the things that are beautiful and sustaining from a shared past, especially the Palestinian-Israeli experience of internal exile. In this way, family is the flower of exile for Raqraq, and the lost village remains in the family. Of course, the ultimate expression of the son's commitment to the father's vision of life, an ember from the old world before exile, is felt but not articulated: "The words never left the son's mouth." Such articulation would be a step too far in the direction of fantasy, and *The Owl Neighborhood*, like all of Dhaher's work, honors reality at a fundamental level.

Works Cited

Darwish, Mahmoud. "Counterpoint: Homage to Edward Said." Trans. Julie Stoker. *Le Monde Diplomatique*. January 2005, http://www.bintjbeil.com/articles/2005/en/0129_darwish.html. Accessed 23 February 2019.

——. "I Belong There." Trans. Munir Akash and Carolyn Forché. *Unfortunately, It Was Paradise*. Ed. Munir Akash and Carolyn Forché. University of California Press. 2013, p. 7.

Fitzgerald, F. Scott. *The Great Gatsby*. Scribner, 2004.

Kashua, Sayed. "Israel Doesn't Want to Be My State." *New York Times*. 30 July 2018, https://www.nytimes.com/2018/07/30/opinion/israel-nationality-law-palestinian-citizens.html. Accessed 23 February 2019.

——. "Why Sayed Kashua Is Leaving Jerusalem and Never Coming Back." *Haaretz*. 4 July 2014, https://www.haaretz.com/.premium-for-sayed-kashua-co-existence-has-failed-1.5254338. Accessed 23 February 2019.

Margalit, Ruth. "An Exile in the Corn Belt: Israeli's Funniest Palestinian Writer Decamps in the Midwest." *New Yorker*. 7 September 2015, https://www.newyorker.com/magazine/2015/09/07/an-exile-in-the-corn-belt. Accessed 23 February 2019.

Said, Edward. "Reflections on Exile." *Reflections on Exile and Other Essays*. Harvard University Press, 2000, pp. 173–186.

3

Palestinians in Lebanon: The Inevitable Misery

IBRAHIM MOHAMAD KARKOUTI

There is no room for Palestinian creativity in Lebanon because Palestinians are refugees! Quite terrifying, isn't it? It is the sad reality, however. This is the price that the displaced Palestinians pay every day because they were expelled and were forced to seek asylum in Lebanon and other Arab countries to escape inevitable death in Palestine. Nevertheless, Palestinians have been able to cope with daily challenges, assimilate to new cultures, thrive, and persist. This article presents a brief analysis of Mazen Ma'arouf's representative works. A young Palestinian poet who lived in Lebanon, Ma'arouf defied and resisted oppression, inequity, and injustice through his writing.

In Lebanon, the most religiously and culturally diverse nation in the Arab world, Palestinians are second-class residents who are not entitled to any rights because they are refugees (Bayoumy). Palestinians are not authorized to join professional syndicates, restricted from working in many fields, barred from owning property and from formal education, and forced to live in camps (Khoury). This should not be surprising, as the Lebanese constitution discriminates against its own people on the basis of religion. For example, the president of the country must always be a Maronite, the prime minister a Sunni, and the head of the parliament a Shiite (Moaddel, Kors, & Garde). When they are confronted by human rights activists who expose the systemic abuses against Palestinian refugees, many Lebanese politicians and policymakers bring up the Palestinian "Right of Return" to justify unjust practices and the lax policies that facilitate discrimination and increase the disparities between locals and foreign residents. More importantly, in the name of preserving "Palestinian Identity," refugees in Lebanon and elsewhere are not allowed to travel to most Arab countries. Indeed, Palestinian refugees continue to suffer this Arab betrayal to the present day. One of the contemporary Palestinian refugee poets in Lebanon who gives voice to the plight of Palestinians in Lebanon is Mazen Ma'arouf.

Ma'arouf was born and raised in Beirut. He was forced to leave Lebanon in 2011 because he criticized the Syrian regime and currently lives in exile in Iceland. In an interview with the Al Jazeera Network, Ma'arouf said, "I wouldn't have been forced to leave Lebanon for criticizing the Syrian regime if I were a Lebanese citizen" (Vilk 1). Ma'arouf's statement makes it evident that Palestinians in Lebanon face double standards. Lebanon not only discriminates against certain religious groups, but also employs biased laws and policies against non-citizens. Simply put, Ma'arouf's daring and thought-provoking poetry was intolerable to a government that does not accept cultural, religious, and political difference.

In his poem "A Colored Pin," Ma'arouf writes:

> It so happens that you find a stiff bird/ nailed with a colored pin/ believing he is perched on a branch/ and that soon rain will fall/ a hand opens the window to rescue him/ from the long waves of coughing that haunt me.

In this poem, Ma'arouf depicts himself as a bird and describes his immediate community as a cage that restricts his freedom. He points out that people do not recognize that they are imprisoned by their own belief systems. This poem expresses Ma'arouf's hope that someday a stranger will liberate his inner soul and set him free.

In his poem "Downtown," Ma'arouf writes:

> My share of sleep:/four hours eleven minutes./I roll my pierced heart/across the bedcover:/it slams into the door,/leaving/a line of mud behind./I believe/a tree/will come one night/and stop/beside the line./Another tree/will follow,/and a third,/a fourth,/a ninth,/ etc./One night/the line will grow/and become a street./One night/ while I'm sleeping/friends will stream/out of my head/and into

the street/to sleep beneath the trees./And I,/one night,/will wake/ from fear of solitude/and follow them.

In this poem, Ma'arouf describes the agony that Palestinians suffer on a daily basis. He implies that his people live in terrible conditions that degrade one's body and soul. He views heaven as the promised savior that will uplift their souls, take away their sins, end their loneliness, overcome self-imposed limitations, and eliminate community-imposed restrictions.

Finally, in his poem "Solitary Confinement on the Seventh Floor," Ma'arouf writes:

> One day, I'll tear off my lips and eat them like candy. One day, I'll rip out my chest because I'm not an orphanage for gathering angels. One day, I'll remove the door and stand in its stead to stop myself from leaving for the hole in the world.

In this poem, Ma'arouf implies that happiness is the product of misery. Also, he expresses his discontent with the unjust circumstances that forced him to leave his memories behind. At the end of the poem, Ma'arouf explains that all places are terrifying except home, and therefore makes a promise that he will return back to his home and never return again to what he describes as "the hole in the world."

Palestine is also the subject of its fair share of Ma'arouf's poetry. According to Ma'arouf, Palestinian society is broken because it lacks an informed and competent citizenry (Irving). In an interview with The Electronic Intifada, the young poet shared, "We don't need to cry. Sure, we'll cry when something happens to one of our people, but we don't need to be covered with this blanket of sadness. The Palestinian people don't need any more emotion, they need minds" (Irving, 15). He wrote the poem "DNA" about Palestine:

> There is only one way/ to scream:/ remembering that you're ... Palestinian. / One way to gaze at your face/ in the bus window:/ with the passing trees/ and the porters who appear/ whenever you stop./ One way to reach the ozone layer:/ lightly, like a balloon./ One way to cry:/ because you really are a bastard. /One way/

to place your hand on your lover's breasts/ and dream:/ of distant things/ like the Louvre/ and a small apartment in a Paris suburb,/ and of so much/ solitude/ and so many books./ One way to die:/ provoke one of the snipers/ in the morning's early hours./ One way to say whore:/ to the whore in your bed./ One way to smoke hash:/ in an elevator, alone,/ at eleven at night./ One way to write a poem:/ miserably, in the bathroom./ One way to scream:/ in the sewer,/ where your face appears/ for a second/ in the shit-filled waters/ to remind you/ of how you're nothing,/ absolutely nothing,/ but a Palestinian.

In this remarkable poem, Ma'arouf explains that facing the reality of one's Palestinian identity is, at bottom, terrifying. He blames himself and his fellow citizens for losing their holy land. Further, he describes the stages of life that Palestinians go through outside their homeland in a very disturbing way. Ma'arouf attributes his discontent with life to the tragedy of the Palestinian diaspora. The fact that Palestinians are refugees in Lebanon is problematic in the sense that it strips them of their basic human rights of public education and healthcare, employment, and prosperity (Monahan). In support of this argument, Elias Khoury, a prominent Lebanese novelist who relentlessly defends Palestinian rights confirms the harsh living conditions of Palestinian refugees in Lebanon. Khoury, a leftist intellectual, is among the very few Christian Lebanese who joined the Lebanese National Movement in its early days. In local and international events, he always seizes the opportunity to expose human rights abuses against Palestinians in Lebanon, the Arab world, and Israel. His own *Gate of the Sun* is considered the greatest novel to confront the Nakba and its consequences. In it, he describes the expulsion of hundreds of thousands of Palestinian refugees during the 1948 war and highlights the humiliation that Palestinians endured as a result of the forced displacement (Silverman). Although Ma'arouf and Khoury come from distinct cultures and are citizens of two different nations, they both fight the same war. The Palestinian Cause is the war that they have dedicated their lives to.

Unlike his Palestinian predecessors who lived in Lebanon (e.g., Mahmoud Darwish, Kamal Nasser, and Ghassan Kanafani), Mazen Ma'arouf integrates both surrealism and fantasy in his work (Hosny). According to Hosny, the secret behind Ma'arouf's acceptance by a wide range of readers is his "balanced narrative rhythm, cinematic description of places and events, and an Arabic language that tends to be simple" (1). In 2017, Ma'arouf published his second collection of stories, *The Rats That Lick a Karate Champion's Ears*. In this volume, he is highly critical of the Lebanese Civil War, but he also writes nostalgically in fiction that draws on his own time in Lebanon (Hosny). Indeed, Ma'arouf's latest publication shows how loyal he is to the country that forced him into exile.

Ma'arouf did not give up on Lebanon. Instead, he kept communicating his love for it through poetry and prose (Hosny). He made a promise to return to honor life in Beirut, commemorate the past, and celebrate the future. Mazen Ma'arouf sets an example of loyalty for Lebanon, even as its own citizens are eager to abandon it. During his time in Lebanon, he created an enduring sense of belonging that few Lebanese could match. Now, the big question is: Will the Lebanese authorities grant him amnesty in return for his dedication and loyalty to the country? Time will tell whether he will be able to write again on Palestine from his balcony in Beirut.

Works Cited

Bayoumy, Yara. "Lebanon urged to treat Palestinian refugees better". *Reuters*. 17 October 2007, https://www.reuters.com/article/us-palestinians-lebanon-rights/lebanon-urged-to-treat-palestinian-refugees-better-idUSL1663278620071017. Accessed 10 March 2018.

Hosny, Mahmoud. "Mazen Maarouf: At the intersection between surrealism and fantasy". *Arabic Literature and Translation*. 23 October 2017, https://arablit.org/2017/10/23/mazen-maarouf-at-the-intersection-between-surrealism-and-fantasy/. Accessed 10 March 2018.

Irving, Sarah. "Palestinians shouldn't be covered in blanket of sadness, says poet". *The Electronic Intifada*. 27 February 2013, https://electronicintifada.net/content/palestinians-shouldnt-be-covered-blanket-sadness-says-poet/12232. Accessed 10 March 2018.

Khour, Lisa. "Palestinians in Lebanon: It's like living in a prison". *Aljazeera*. 16 December 2017, https://www.aljazeera.com/news/2017/12/palestinians-lebanon-living-prison-171215114602518.html. Accessed 10 March 2018.

Maarouf, Mzen. "Downtown". Trans. Kareem James Abu-Zeid and by Nathalie Handal. *Words without Borders, The Online Magazine for International Literature*. April 2014, https://www.wordswithoutborders.org/article/downtown. Accessed 27 Jan. 2019.

——. "DNA". Trans. Kareem Abu-Zeid & N. Handal Trans. *Guernica*. 1 August 2014, https:// www.guernicamag.com/dna/. Accessed 27 Jan. 2019.

——. "Six poems". Trans. Jassim. Mohamad. *Literature Across Frontier*. 2014, https://www. lit-across-frontiers.org/transcript/six-poems/. Accessed 27 Jan. 2019.

——. "Solitary confinement on the seventh floor". Trans. Kareem James Abu-Zeid and by Nathalie Handal. *Words without Borders, The Online Magazine for International Literature*. May 2015, https://www.wordswithoutborders.org/article/solitary-confinement-on-the-seventh-floor. Accessed 27 Jan. 2019.

Moaddel, Mansour., Kors, Jean., Garde, Johan. (2012). *Sectarianism and counter-sectarianism in Lebanon*. Population Studies Center Research Report 12-757, University of Chicago. May 2012. https://www.psc.isr.umich.edu/pubs/pdf/rr12-757.pdf. Accessed 27 Jan. 2019.

Monahan, Meghan. "Treatment of Palestinian refugees in Lebanon". *Human Rights Brief*. 2 February 2015. http://hrbrief.org/2015/02/treatment-of-palestinian-refugees-in-lebanon/. Accessed 27 Jan. 2019.

Silverman, Jacob. "Elias Khoury: Profile of the essential Arab novelist today". *Daily Beast*. 8 March 2012, https://www.thedailybeast.com/elias-khoury-profile-of-the-essential-arab-novelist-today. Accessed 27 Jan. 2019.

Vilk, Roxana. "Mazen Maarouf: Handmade". *Aljazeera* 11 April 2014, https://www.aljazeera. com/programmes/poetsofprotest/2012/08/2012829111914434307.html.

Credits

4

Palestinian Literature: A Political Psychology Approach

SERCAN CANBOLAT

Introduction

The provenances of ethnic and religious conflict in the Middle East are deep-seated and convoluted. The 1948 calamity diffused the Palestinian community throughout the broader Middle East and beyond, threatening to destroy the social fabric of Palestine. Today there are almost one million and eight hundred thousand Palestinians within Israel while roughly four million and eight hundred thousand Palestinians live in the Gaza Strip and West Bank (Abu Toameh). It is reported that close to another six million live in the Diaspora territories, most as exiles in Syria, Lebanon, and Jordan, just across from what was once their perennial home (Tessler 9). The dispersed Palestinian community has waged a long-lasting battle for recognition and identity since the 1948 crisis.

The oppressive conditions dictated by the Israeli government have engendered a strong sense of Palestinian national identity among the dispersed Palestinian groups. Individual Palestinians have long resided in a contested national territory controlled by a foreign power, and therefore their national consciousness has been shaped towards the goal of expelling the foreign oppressor and establishing an independent state on the historical homeland.

A Post-Traumatic Appraisal of Palestinian Resistance Literature

The main dilemma for the trauma-stricken Palestinian society is that their dispersal across the region and world stymies the longed-for formation of a common nation-state even as alienation from the homeland and statelessness continues to stoke a profound nationalism. In some ways, the stateless Palestinian community and its heightened Arab nationalism have parallels with those of the ethnic Kurds in the Middle East (Tolovan 5). That said, the trauma endured by the Palestinian community has been exacerbated by the historical fact that the national community that has occupied Palestinian territory was itself the victim of one of world history's most horrendous persecutions and genocides. For this reason, the dispersed and traumatized Palestinian society has always had to come to grips with the fact that "they are the victims of victims" (Cleary 187).

A dearth of Palestinian resistance literature has never been the problem. Palestinians have risen against attempts to destroy them as a society with notable resilience and might since the Arab Revolts in the late 1930s. Nevertheless, territorial fragmentation and demographic diffusion have taken its toll on the Palestinian community across the Middle East. At different times, the mandate of the revolt against Israel has been shouldered by differing segments of the Palestinian society. For instance, it was mainly the refugee communities in the Diaspora that waged guerrilla wars against Israel in the 1970s and 1980s. In the 1990s, however, the leadership role shifted to civilian resistance (intifada) in the occupied Palestinian lands.

Moreover, the Palestinians within Israel have tried to resist state discrimination for decades. This internal civil-rights movement is viewed as only tangential to the ultimate nation-building mission spearheaded by other segments of the Palestinian nation. Consequently, while the mandates of revolt and resistance have been transferred from one fraction of the community to another at different times, it has always been difficult to incorporate and coordinate these different struggles toward the overarching goal of an independent Palestinian nation.

It is in the context of this hardened national struggle that the development of Palestinian resistance literature should be assessed.

Resistance literature does not necessarily trump other arts in the struggle for Palestinian nationhood, but it remains true that when Palestinians long to express their national mission in a solid form, it is to resistance literature that they turn their gaze. Accordingly, the fiction of writers, including Naji Dhaher, can play a major role in the national struggle. As prominent Palestinian leader Yasser Arafat once noted: "Our Palestinian, Lebanese, and Arab poets and writers have composed odes and articles which have become part of the siege ... But I am waiting for more; I am waiting *for the novel* which will penetrate Arab public opinion and not just break the windows of the house" (190).

Notably, even some of the most famous Arab poets have suggested the precedence of fiction over poetry as the major genre of modern Arab political expression. In 1982, Mahmoud Darwish, one of the pioneering national poets of Palestine, asserted that "while the poet was once everything to Arabic culture: journalist, professor, leader, the form to which I most aspire to fulfill now is in prose. There is no one in this age that I envy more than the novelists and story tellers because the novel can expand to include everything ... In the novel you can sing and speak poetry, prose, ideas, and practically everything" (190).

Likewise, Fadwa Tuqan, a noted Palestinan poet, argued in an interview in 1989 that the sustained demand of publicizing the Palestinian struggle requires a literary form more spacious in its scope than poetry. She maintained that "the poem is no longer capable of accommodating the riches of the *intifada* experience in all its aspects. Poetry alludes, but oblique reference does not seem to be enough at the moment ... I dream of a bigger work, a work that can accommodate my vision of those great happenings more than the poem can, and I have become haunted with the idea of writing a novel that embraces all aspects of the *intifada*" (191).

As these notable Arab poets suggest, stories, such as those collected in this volume, help individual Palestinians dream of a final recovery from their long trauma. When they can dream of the fiction that can include everything, Palestinians will be able to use prose forms to imaginatively conceive a national belonging that is yet to be realized politically. Recent scholarship on resistance literature points to the commonality between the modern nation-state, which aims to incorporate all the people of a certain homeland in one unified historical account, and the great modern realist literary texts whose authors compass multiple characters and multiple small plots in a single overarching narrative (Hallaj 69).

In one of his major works, Edward Said compares the Egyptian realist writers to their Lebanese and Palestinian counterparts. Said maintains that for Palestinian and Lebanese story-tellers and novelists, the completeness and linearity of Egyptian Naguib Mahfouz's realist prose-style texts have proved "maddeningly, frustratingly *not* possible" (Said 139). The encyclopedic solidity, textual density, and thick description of Mahfouz's realist prose, as noted by Said, rest on the literary sources of a territorially stable and well-integrated national society. However, Said asserts in his article "Afterword" that for the Lebanese society whose nation-state imploded in the 1980s and for the Palestinian nation whose country vanished from world maps in the aftermath of 1948, prose forms are rather risky and highly problematic. Said adds that in the trauma-ridden and fragmented political conditions of Lebanese and Palestinian societies, the absolute solidity of Mahfouz's classical realist prose cannot be easily found and replicated. He points out that in Lebanese and Palestinian political culture, the prose-style literary text, such as the novel, "exists largely as a form recording its own impossibility" (140).

Conclusion

Many of the psychological questions within Palestinian resistance literature can be conceived in terms of their wider macro-level and structural determinants in the colonial and underdeveloped world generally. Particularly, it can be argued that there are three major political and psychological questions that call for the attention of Palestinian resistance literature.

First, one of the fundamental aims of Palestinian resistance writing is to propose a Palestinian counter-narrative vis-à-vis the more established and organized Israeli version. Israel was the winner in the 1948 traumatic event, and the Israeli government has maintained its dominance ever since. Additionally, Israeli writers and scholars enjoy a close relationship with the Western world in general and the US government in particular. These relationships grant Israeli narrators control over the image of Palestinians in the international mass media. Therefore, the authoritative version of Israeli–Palestinian relations is largely defined in Israeli and US terms, at least outside the Middle East. Hence, one of the great challenges of Palestinian resistance literature is to prevent the suppression of the Palestinian version of events in the marketplace of ideas and narratives. That is, Palestinian writers must write Palestinians back into history.

Second, because the Palestinian homeland has been largely occupied by Israeli settlements, which have literally renamed the homeland in Hebrew, many Palestinian writers and poets are engaged in what James Clifford has called "textual rescue" or what Edward Said describes as "a process to reclaim, rename, and re-inhabit the alienated landscape through the imagination" (Clifford 237). The recitations of litanies of lost villages and towns in Palestinian prose, including Dhaher's fiction, is one of the most striking examples of the textual rescue enterprise.

Next, given the apocalyptic nature of post-1948 Palestinian history, much of Palestinian resistance literature struggles to come to grips with a chronic trauma that evokes what Fredric Jameson has described as "the hurt of history" (102). Political calamity of the magnitude suffered by the Palestinians inevitably exacts an enormous human suffering; it induces a sense of individual and collective rage, frustration, despair, humiliation, and recrimination. One of the functions of resistance literature, therefore, is to vocalize the work of mourning, which is a required and inevitable part of any long-term process of historical recovery from collective trauma. Moreover, as Edward Said noted in the article "Arabic Prose and Prose Fiction since 1948," the 1948 events represented a devastating political catastrophe for the Palestinians, which meant that "Arabs everywhere were forced additionally to confront as their own problem, and taking an especially provocative form, one of the greatest and still unsolved problems of Western civilization, the Jewish question" (10). Said argues that the Israeli victory in 1948 triggered a barrage of unprecedented challenges to the entire notion of a collective Arab national identity and to the larger project of Arab modernization, thus causing problems that not only Palestinians but Arabs everywhere have been forced to address.

According to Said, the 1948 traumatic shock needs to be grasped not only as a human tragedy but also as a shattering crisis in narrative within the entire Arab world as well. Said forcefully argues that for the Palestinian author "nothing in his (sic) history, that is, in the repertory or vocabulary provided to him by his historical experience, gave him an adequate method for representing the Palestinian drama to himself" (15). One of the tasks that the proponents of resistance literature should consider is that of making sense of the 1948 traumatic shock, not only of analyzing and reporting the human misery it engendered, but also of determining its meaning and significance for the Arab world.

In this context, Dhaher's short stories vocalize the pride, anger and determination of Palestinian resistance. In his trauma-laden stories, Dhaher evokes the persistent themes of Palestinian resistance literature, which include identity, nostalgia, love, desire, even death. Dhaher interrogates Palestinian national identity and vocalizes the individual struggles of ordinary Palestinians. Dhaher's personal background as a Palestinian is integral to his work. This fraught but enduring identity is manifest throughout the short stories and novella collected by Abu Rabia in *The Exiled Prophet*. In this volume, it is clear that despite mean circumstances Dhaher manages to celebrate the life of exile.

Work Cited

Abu Toameh, Khaled. "Palestinian census: 4.7 million in West Bank and Gaza Strip". *Times of Israel*. March 28 2018, https://www.timesofisrael.com/palestinian-census-4-7-million-in-west-bank-and-gaza-strip/. Accessed 16 April 2018.

Barakat, Halim. *Days of Dust*. Three Continent Press, Washington, D.C. 1974.

Cleary, Joe. *Literature, Partition and the Nation-state: Culture and Conflict in Ireland, Israel and Palestine*. Cambridge University Press, 2002.

Clifford, James, George E., Marcus, and Kim, Fortun. *Writing Culture: The Poetics and Politics of Ethnography*. University of California Press, 2010.

Hallaj, Muhammad. "Recollections of the Nakba through a Teenager's Eyes." *Journal of Palestine Studies 38*, no. 1, 2008, pp.66–73. doi:10.1525/jps.2008,38.1.

Jameson, Fredric. *The Political Unconscious Narrative as a Socially Symbolic Act*. Ithaca: Cornell University Press, 2014.

Khoury, Elias, Maia Tabet, and Edward W. Said. *Little Mountain*. Manchester, England: Carcanet, 1989.

Said, Edward W. *Culture and Imperialism.* *London:* Vintage Digital, 2014.

—. *Reflections on Exile and Other Essays.* Cambridge, MA: Harvard University Press, 2002.

Tessler, Mark A. *A History of the Israeli-Palestinian Conflict.* *Bloomington:* Indiana University Press, 2009.

Tölölyan, Khachig. "The Nation-State and Its Others: In Lieu of a Preface." *Diaspora: A Journal of Transnational Studies* 1, 1. 1991. p. 3–7. doi:10.1353/dsp.1991.0008.

5
Biography of Naji Dhaher

HAZZA ABU RABIA

Personal Background

It was a cold night when Naji Dhaher was born on January 8, 1951, in a building left behind by the British forces atop Mount Seikh, which overlooks Nazareth. This mountain is now called *"Har Yonah."* Dhaher's birthplace is in the present-day Jewish city of Nazareth Illit, which was built for the new Israeli settlers in the 1950s.

His family had already moved several times after being displaced from their village of Sirin in the area of Bisan in the Jordan Valley district. Sirin is one of the twenty-nine villages in Bisan, which was destroyed by the Israeli Occupation forces in 1948. Perhaps because of its proximity to the Jordan Valley and border, most of Dhaher's extended family fled to the city of Irbid in Jordan. His immediate family was among a small group of villagers who remained within historical Palestine.

Dhaher's mother often told her son that she swaddled him tightly and resumed her daily housework hours after his birth. His family was displaced and scattered after the Nakba to every corner in historical Palestine and the neighboring countries. His parents moved and lived in many villages during their vagrancy, including Taiba al-Zubiyya village and Kafr Misr in Jezreel Valley. They moved from town to town until they settled in Nazareth in 1950.

In Nazareth, the Dhahers described themselves as refugees and were known as such. Their first shelter in Nazareth was the home of a generous woman who took them in when they had no place to go. They moved from this woman's home to the abandoned military building on Mount Seikh where Naji was born. It is not clear how his father knew about this empty building. According to Dhaher, his father either discovered it himself or someone suggested he use it as a shelter for his family.

After Naji's birth, the family moved to a rented house in the market area in the old town of Nazareth, a desirable location. But they did not remain there long. They soon moved again, this time to the village of Daburiya where they stayed for two years, at which point they moved back to Nazareth. It was there, in a rented house in the eastern neighborhood that Dhaher began to understand what was going on around him. He was a young man when his family moved to the Safafreh neighborhood in Nazareth. Safafreh consisted mainly of displaced families from the nearby village of Safourieh. Naji's parents managed to buy a small piece of land and built a house. Some of his family members still live there today.

Naji was so precocious as a child that his mother called him an old man when he was only five years old. His mother would caution her friends and neighbors to watch what they say in front of the "old man" because her young son understood all that was going on around him.

Dhaher developed a strong personality and an independent streak during his difficult and unhappy childhood. He recalls, for example, how his family would take advantage of the special dispensation offered on Israeli Independence Day, which permitted them to visit towns that were otherwise off-limits. The stubborn youth refused to accompany his family, insisting that "the day of their independence is the day of our catastrophe." He would spend the holiday contemplating the miseries of displacement.

From an early age, Naji hoped to compensate his parents for their displacement from Sirin. When his mother asked him what he wanted to be when he grew up, he told her that he wanted to be a writer. To his mother this meant sitting in front of the Muscovite administration building in Nazareth every day to write letters and fill out forms for poor, illiterate peasants. Naji answered her that he wanted to write stories. When she asked him what he meant, he told her that he wanted to write tales of the suffering his mother had endured since her expulsion from her village by the Israelis.

In his childhood, he heard many stories from an elderly blind woman who lived in a house not far from their rented home. These tales fascinated him. He would seek her out before school in the morning and again in the evening. At school, he would share these stories as if he were a playwright, distributing roles to each of his schoolmates to act out.

He began to feel that he had a gift that he had to bring into the light. He would use his gift to challenge cruelty and injustice. He would shout in the faces of his oppressors: "Enough injustice and enough cruelty! You treat us like burned ashes at life's margins. The hearts that you torment belong to your brothers, your fellow human beings."

From the stories of this old woman, young Naji adopted two principles that he was not fully aware of at the time. One is that his writing would reject injustice in all its forms; the other is that as a human being he would play a role in the restoration of justice in the world. These commitments would give his creative writing purpose. To this day, Dhaher believes that the creative writer must spread happiness among his fellow human beings and give voice to their suffering.

During elementary school, he discovered the Egyptian writer Kamel Kilani, whom he considered a treasure. This writer drew his themes from the local legends of his Arabic heritage. Because of this shared heritage, Dhaher was attached to his works and read his books with great desire. But what was amazing to Dhaher is that Kilani's books are full of adventures in which the protagonists confront the ruthless world. Kilani wrote in a fine formal Arabic, which made him unique. Kalani's texts included footnotes that glossed the meanings of the difficult words at the bottom of the page, and these definitions were gold to the young writer who eagerly enriched his vocabulary. Young Naji had discovered the world of books and began to imagine the library as a kind of heaven.

First Literary Education

From the moment he discovered the richness of language and the beautiful world of literature, Dhaher became obsessed. But he faced a practical problem: Where could he find more books? In the 1950s and 1960s, the Palestinian community was under martial law and disconnected from their larger environment, the Arab world. This meant that books were scarce. But even if books were available, where would he get the money to buy them? These limitations made Dhaher into an opportunistic reader. One time he found a pile of scattered papers. When he collected them and read them, he found that he had read a whole book *The Disadvantages of the Ministers* by Abu Hayyan Tawhidi. He also read a collection of stories called *The Library of Humor* by the pioneering Palestinian writer Khalil Beidas.

His never-ending search led him to a library at the *Histadrut* House in Nazareth, named after the American artist Frank Sinatra.[1] He worked his way through the library book by book. He read everything: literature, history, philosophy, music, and art. He did not simply read but took notes and analyzed what he read.

In this library, he read hundreds of novels in the "Pocketbooks" and "World Novels" imprints of well-known books translated into Arabic. Sometimes, he would read two or three novels in a day. His senses told him that he had discovered a beautiful world. Inspired by his reading, he challenged himself to reach for what is simultaneously subjective and universal in his own writing. He still reads voraciously and considers books among his dearest companions.

Early Literary Career

Dhaher started writing as a teenager in the mid-sixties. His first story was about a traveling salesman who was psychologically broken and depressed. All doors were closed in his face; he wanted to open only one, but never could.

In this period, Dhaher wrote many stories, which he published with some reluctance. He even tried to publish some under a false name to know the true opinion of the people around him. He knew that if his friends read them, they would either welcome them because their author was their friend, or they would criticize him harshly out of envy or jealousy. In this context, he recalls a chance encounter with the late

---

1   The *Histadrut* or the General Organization of Workers in Israel is Israel's national trade union center, representing the majority of trade unionists in the State of Israel. It was established in the early 1920s and offers services to working-class families.

journalist Mohammed Sharif, who stopped Dhaher and a friend, with whom Sharif was acquainted. Sharif and this friend talked about Dhaher's writings, although Sharif did not realize that Dhaher was right there with them. Dhaher emerged feeling confident and proud: A well-known journalist was asking, "Who is this Naji?"

He continued to write and publish with diffidence and a low profile until 1968, when he wrote a beautiful story called "The Last Word," and submitted it to the monthly magazine *Al Jadid*. He was surprised at the end of the month to find his story in the magazine. He told himself that the journey of a thousand miles had finally begun, and from that day, he made every effort to improve as a writer. Since then, he has never slept as other people do. He started to read and write with a new intensity, telling himself whoever wants to achieve something in this life must give up many things.

His published writings now number some forty books. Many of his short stories have been published in collected volumes. In 2000, he received the Creativity Award, and in the same year, two literature magazines, *Al Sharq* and *Al Mawakeb*, devoted special editions to Dhaher and his work. He feels that his life's dream has come true.

PART 2

Selected Short Stories

NAJI DHAHER

1

Klaris

She woke up one morning full of joy. From bed, she moved the curtain aside and looked at the city. The houses were still the same houses— the tiled roofs, the buildings that have sprouted here and there, the tall structures and the small houses besides them, the old mixed with the new, so that you could no longer distinguish between them unless you were a resident of the old city. She had seen this same view thousands of times, maybe tens of thousands, but it had never seemed so magnificent.

She felt forty years younger than she was. Back when she was twenty-five, she would tell the streets "Get up from your sleep," and they would rise up and would not sleep again until she asked them to. She was a little nervous and uncertain about the day she had planned, so she summoned the joy that came from the past, and it covered her with its glory and spread out until it flooded the houses, and the city, once again, rose with her.

She removed the cover from her skinny body, put her foot on the dewy floor. She felt the moisture that the open window let in, and soon the warmth returned to her.

It is 6 o'clock, and it is Sunday; her daughter and her granddaughter are still asleep. She is thinking about the city of Haifa, which is far away from Nazareth, but close to her heart. For a moment, she considered waking her daughter and her granddaughter, but soon changed her mind and went back to bed. "Let them sleep a little bit more," she thought to herself. "Today is Sunday."

She returned to her bed. Her hand moved instinctively to her heart where she placed the letter that came forty years late, but nevertheless

Naji Dhaher, "Klaris," trans. Hazza Abu Rabia. Translated with permission by Naji Dhaher.

filled her sky and the sky of Nazareth with joy. She put her head on the pillow, and half of her nakedness appeared in the light of the morning defying the years. The half-open curtain let the morning air into the quiet room, which was filled by the color of the mountains and the scent of beauty. The letter came very late, but nevertheless lighted the universe and made Nazareth much more beautiful than it had been. It rekindled a beauty that illuminated everything around her, and so she said to herself what he said to her forty years ago: "If you want to see the world's beauty you must be beautiful before anything." His words had lit a longing inside her. So long ago, she had closed her eyes and imagined the future: Their children playing on the beach, her lover hugging her in the sunlight, and Klaris smiling and saying: "Not in front of the boys." He would answer: "What's wrong? Do we steal?"

The morning moisture brought her back to herself, to her letter, to the ruthless frenzy of the present, and to the future that would be full of hope. The sad words in his late letter transported her to the past. The sad words filled her present with joy, what beautiful words he wrote: "Come, I want to see you. My soul was with you for these forty years, but I chose to stay here in Haifa. I did not want to be an obstacle in your life ... but these are my last days. I must see you and your daughter and your granddaughter."

This letter thrilled her. She had not received any letters for many years, except the letters that came to her by mistake from the tax and social security offices. Even those were actually received by her husband, and after his death were received by her daughter. This letter, his letter, had not been delivered to her daughter. The postman handed it directly to her. The envelope read: "To be delivered only to Mrs. Klaris." She opened the letter with trembling hands and touched the past that she thought would never come back. It returned to tell her that something was not over and that the man who filled her life and her soul was still alive in apartment no. 12 on Stanton Street in Haifa. Once she read the letter, she surrendered to the numbness that swept through her body, and for a few minutes she was oblivious to her surroundings.

It was an unusual Sunday. Liveliness filled the house. She heard steps moving in the next room. Then the door of her room opened, and her daughter's face appeared. She was about twenty-five, the very age when Klaris had fled from Haifa with her parents and her relatives, in the wave of panic that followed the occupying gangs. Her daughter smiled warmly. Her husband had immigrated to Canada two years ago, and since that day she kissed her daughter, little Klaris, each morning before going to work, and on her way back home she brought food and other necessities.

Klaris greeted her daughter and asked in a whispering voice: "Where is the little Klaris?" Since the day her granddaughter was born, six years ago, she felt a powerful connection to her namesake.

The daughter said: "She is asleep, but I will wake her in a bit. We should leave early because there are more busses and cabs on Sunday morning than at noon."

Klaris did not respond, and her daughter did not repeat her suggestion. She did not need to. For the past two years since the immigration of her daughter's husband, Klaris had listened to her without ever interrupting.

Klaris dragged her sixty-five years behind her and leaned on her daughter for support as she boarded the bus, which was surprisingly full. Klaris was relieved to find an empty seat in the middle of the bus. She sat down and gathered her black jacket under her thighs to leave room for her daughter to sit beside her. When she and her daughter had settled, she discovered that the little Klaris was still standing. Klaris found another empty seat in the next row and said to her granddaughter: "Sit down, my baby."

The little girl was silent. Her grandmother turned her head and noticed that the empty seat was partly covered by the clothes of the passenger in the adjoining seat. To draw this rider's attention, Klaris spoke gently: "Now sit down, my love, and your aunt will move her clothes." Little Klaris sat dutifully, and the bus headed toward Haifa and the past.

On the day that she fled with her family from Haifa, they were pursued by fear. Zionist gangs were terrorizing the people to drive them from the city at any cost. Their last days at home brought one shock after another, news of killing, the torture of passersby, and the abuse of innocent people. Klaris tried to offer something to the revolutionaries, not only because her lover was among them, but because she believed in the revolution and freedom. She understood that every important thing in life carries a price.

She was going to see him, to see the rebels, who held onto different parts of the city. She was taking them food, medicine, and bandages that she bought with the little money that she had. She was going to meet them there. She was delighted to return to her beloved. Her father and family did not ask where she went, no matter how long she was absent from home, yet they were indeed worried. No one asked where she was going. Everything was clear to them, but no one wanted to talk about it. Everyone was afraid of the occupying gangs, and the rebels provided warmth and security to the neighborhoods that were still under their control. There she could find him still. The more shells exploded, and the more shots clattered in the streets nearby, the tighter they held one another and the more they felt that they were loyal both to the city and to their love. It was as if imminent death were uniting them, somehow making them even closer to one another. At first, he was filled with hope. He told her about the sacrifices of the revolutionaries during the night. No one complained, and when one in the resistance became weak because he had young children, no one slandered him. Instead, they steadfastly manned their positions, saying we may die, yet our children will live. As the resistance dwindled and things looked their bleakest, she continued to bring supplies, but now she clung to him with a desperate ferocity, as if she could never hold him close enough.

On the day he felt that the city would fall into the hands of the occupiers, he held her to his chest and wept. He told her:

"If this night passes and the city does not fall, it will be for us forever." But the night passed, and the city fell street by street until entire neighborhoods had fallen. The residents of the city were leaving, terrified by rumors of killings and rape and by the bodies scattered in the streets. Suddenly, she found herself packing. She and her family gathered those valuables light enough to carry and fled in the direction of Nazareth.

Most of all they carried their sorrows. They stopped, at last, at a small house on Mount Farah in Nazareth. All the while, she tried to follow the news on the resistance. But she had no luck, as everyone had a different story. Some told her that her lover was dead, killed with the last rebels. She managed to sustain hope during the first two years, but after more time passed, and her father died, she still had no word from her lover. She surrendered, at last, to the long heavy days. When the chance came to marry a reasonable man, she did, and she stayed in Mount Farah. She gave birth to her daughter. Her daughter married and gave birth to her little Klaris, and her daughter's husband immigrated to Canada. And now, after forty years, here he is, her one true lover coming back to her long after her hope had died. He wanted to see her and her daughter. He wanted to see the past that had not or could not die. She asked herself: "What is his story? Did he immigrate and come back to his city? Why didn't he contact me? Did he get married or did he stay single waiting to return?" She did not find an answer to her questions. She forgot the intervening years that had come and passed so suddenly, and she was back again in the first days of love, and the young lover she once was returned to her and said, "Here are the days of your youth."

In Haifa, she did not ask anyone to show her to Stanton Street, apartment number 12. She told her daughter and her granddaughter to wait for her as she asked about an old friend. She left them near the bus station and ran towards him. The old buildings, the cries of the vendors in the street, and the many changes in the city did not faze her. She ran towards him, towards his house. She no longer thought of the questions she'd ask; she thought only of seeing him. She came to challenge the long years of distance and abandonment, years of fear, anticipation and hope. After years of anguish, she would re-unite with him on Stanton Street. She would prevail over the years and she would see him again.

When she approached apartment no. 12, she heard an unfamiliar scream that called to mind death and its sorrows. No one knows death like her. Death was faster than her. She saw a young man about the age of her daughter, about the same age as she was in the days before Haifa fell. The stricken young man was peering through the door of apartment number 12. He looked like her lover. He could probably be him! She recoiled from the sudden shock and turned back only to realize that she was not forty years late, but an hour, or perhaps a few minutes. She stopped in her tracks, put her head between her hands, and cried. Now she knew that everything was over.

She found her daughter and her granddaughter where she had left them. When the little Klaris saw her grandmother, she shouted at her: "Grandma, where is your girlfriend? Why didn't you introduce us to her?"

Klaris hugged her and told her: "We will go to her, but not today."

2

The Clever

The village of the clever Sirini (al-Shater al-Sirini) is situated in the northwestern part of the city of Nazareth. Its distinctive location was the main reason that the clever Sirini channeled his creativity to a single musical instrument: the flute. His playing incited happiness in the heart of the village community, including Sit al-Husn, the lady of beauty.

But how did Sit al-Husn get to know al-Shater? That story was told much later. She was acquainted with him one day when she listened to his playing. Back then she was in the early stages of her life. As soon as she lent an ear to his tune, she was dazzled. She had no other choice. While her long black hair flew back, she ran from the other side of the village to the center where he played his instrument, and she was rapt by the enchanting scene of people, trees, fruit and stone.

Sit al-Husn was sitting far from al-Shater al-Sirini, but his music closed the distance between them. What a lovely song! He made Sirini's skies beautiful and enchanting. After the audience dispersed, al-Shater, a young man with no beard, approached Sit al-Husn and played the flute for her alone. It was the most charming melody of his entire life. It seemed at that moment as if he found someone from the villages whom he would like to play for, the one he had dreamt of since he began playing as a child. Sit al-Husn felt that she had just met the man of her dreams and continued to sing his melody until she knew its secrets. Thus, she knew al-Shater now, even if he was only one of the seven million and three hundred thousand musicians in the world. Al-Shater al-Sirini and Sit al-Husn walked together in the path of life. From then

Naji Dhaher, "The Clever," trans. Hazza Abu Rabia. Translated with permission by Naji Dhaher.

on, they were inseparable. They built a house in a peaceful village overlooking the Jordan Valley, and they stayed in that house for a long time.

They began a new chapter in their lives in this period of joy and stability. These were their sweetest and most beautiful days. In the mornings, al-Shater al-Sirini ventured into the wide world for their livelihood, while Sit al-Husn stayed in the house combing her long and dark hair, waiting for her Shater to return.

When al-Shater came back in the evening, he needed only to play his special melody for his beloved wife, and immediately he would find her before him and, moments later, in his embrace.

This is how life was in the world of beautiful music, until one day, in the middle of May 1948, when al-Shater al-Sirini returned to his village, singing his special song for his Sit al-Husn. This time Sit al-Husn did not receive him as usual.

Al-Shater was frantic. He searched the village in vain and saw its destruction with his own eyes. Water buckets were everywhere, bundles of garlic lay in the streets, and doors were scattered in all directions, torn from their houses.

All al-Shater al-Sirini could see was devastation. He searched for Sit al-Husn to no avail.

Al-Shater realized with his artist's intuition that a catastrophe had occurred. What happened was terrible, yet he did not despair. He sought Sit al-Husn throughout the mountains and deserts of the world.

Al-Shater looked and searched, perhaps he would find his Sit al-Husn or at least her trace, but as the weeks went by it seemed that she had simply vanished. Al-Shater played all the melodies he knew to call Sit al-Husn, but only his echo replied.

Al-Shater al-Sirini combed through every corner of the country, but he found no clue to Sit al-Husn's whereabouts. His quest eventually brought him to a fortress that he had never seen before. He told himself: This is *Masada* castle; maybe this is *the* castle of *Masada*.

Jaded and exhausted, Al-Shater lay down at the foot of one of the castle's tall towers and sang a sad melody. It was a song full of sorrows and losses. He was asking himself if he had lost his Sit al-Husn forever.

Suddenly, al-Shater's hand touched black hair dark as the night; he realized that it was Sit al-Husn's hair. The feeling that he thought was gone forever came rushing back to him. Al-Shater did not hesitate to climb the hair, and he found his love imprisoned in a chamber at the top of the tower. Al-Shater did not ask what happened. It was clear that enemies had stormed his village of Sirin during his absence and left his village in desolation when they kidnapped Sit al-Husn.

Al-Shater al-Sirini and Sit al-Husn were then trapped in the citadel, and they were surrounded by the tanks, planes, border guards and combat soldiers that gathered outside. What could they do to get out of this besieged fortress?

Al-Shater grabbed his flute and played a stunning piece. The attack stopped at once. The siege was over. Inside the castle and outside its walls, their enemies were all asleep. Then, al-Shater and his lover went out and left the destruction and its signs behind. When the two returned to their village, the first thing they did was rebuild what the invaders destroyed. They reinstalled the doors on the houses, put the garlic bundles together, and restored the water buckets to their places. They became lanterns lighting the way for other returning villagers and for new visitors and guests.

The old life returned to the village very slowly after the catastrophe, but now it is as vibrant as before, maybe even better. Once the village was restored to life, the lovers took precautions so that the Nakba would not happen again. Al-Shater and Sit al-Husn agreed after a few days of contemplation that she had to learn al-Shater al-Sirini's musical melodies. With her lover as teacher, she learned quickly, and now whenever the enemies send their planes and missiles towards the village for another invasion, Sit al-Husn plays her flute and forces the war jets back to where they came from.

3

A Few Hours in Heaven

My mother returned exhausted from her job of washing clothes for rich people, while my father, my uncle and I sat on the floor of the house that we rented in the old neighborhood in the city of Nazareth, waiting for the mercy of heaven. My mother was feeling blue. Ever since our family was expelled from our homeland village, poverty had afflicted us like a demonic beast. When our family fled, we took refuge in Nazareth. My mother was forced to beg rich families in town for work. Finally, she found a job in one of the mansions in a posh neighborhood. The narrow doors of subsistence cracked opened, and so did the doors of anguish.

My father and uncle looked for work in the city to no avail. No employer would hire them because of their age and the fragility of their old bones. I, the youngest in the family and the fifth son, tearfully watched the scenes of daily torment and the heated arguments between my mother, father, and uncle.

Each day, my mother prepared simple, quick meals with the food she brought home. When she called us to breakfast, we ate as if we had not seen food for a long time. As I watched my mother endure the daily hardships of our new life, I wished that I was born strong enough to work so I could spare my family nights of suffering and days of misery.

One morning, when my father and uncle were about to finish eating, my mother told them: "You have to start looking for a job immediately, rather than tomorrow." My uncle looked at her with curious eyes and wondered about this new urgency. She knew well that they looked for work every day and that this endless search amounted to nothing again and again. My mother looked straight in their eyes, which were red and full of rage, and spoke with a sorrow we had never heard before: "My

Naji Dhaher, "A Few Hours in Heaven," trans. Hazza Abu Rabia. Translated with permission by Naji Dhaher.

employer laid me off. The lady of the house didn't trust her husband, so she wanted me out." The moment she finished her sentence, my father and my uncle raised their frail bodies from the floor and grabbed sticks. They left the muddy old house and headed for the garage area, the central square of Nazareth.

I followed my father and uncle for a while before watching them disappear in the distance. They were men when they left our village, but now they were two strange, thin ghosts walking on the rough land of Nazareth, leaning on their sticks. I wanted badly to help them, but I did not know how. I gazed in all directions, searching for something that could protect them from their painful needs. My thin father and uncle stopped at the garage offering themselves as commodities of labor. The employers examined my father and uncle by shaking them aggressively, then chose others who were well-nourished and full of strength.

My family was tormented by this wretched life in Nazareth, but I took refuge in distant gardens dreamt of by my family but never touched by their exiled feet. I was lost in this old dream when an idea popped into my head, and I immediately pursued it.

I ran after my father and uncle and stopped in front of them like a child who longs to be a giant. They noticed my determined expression and demanded I tell them what I was up to. With surprising confidence, I announced that I had a solution to our problem. My uncle's and father's eyes flashed, and they asked, "What is the solution?" I told them: "Follow me and you will see." My father smiled and looked at my uncle. I started walking and they followed. I felt them look at me as if I were suddenly reborn as a young man and, therefore, could finally help. They walked behind me, and I guessed their thoughts. Did they think that in my daily tour of the neighborhood I had found the treasure of their dreams? Did they think that I would lead them to it? Maybe, but I continued to walk, and they continued to follow.

When I stopped in the rich neighborhood where my mother had worked until that morning, I asked my companions to stay outside a house surrounded by a singing garden. Its yellow and green citrus trees smiled at us. Not far away, the apple and pear trees were waving. The garden looked like God's paradise on earth. I looked at my father and uncle, and I saw in their eyes a tremendous desire to eat the beautiful, inviting fruit. Then I put my plan into action. I approached the gate of the house and knocked on the door. A maid resembling my mother answered and raised her eyebrows at me. Her eyes clearly flashed her desire to kick a beggar from the door. She pulled the door back and was about to close it harshly in my face.

Then I heard the voice of a man, around my father's age, coming from inside the house. I understood from his attire that he was the owner of the house. The man pushed his servant away and stared at me for a few moments. I admit that I did not like his face, and I felt rather uncomfortable. He asked me what I wanted. I told him with a firm voice: "Do you want someone who can work in your garden, to clean the dead grass from around the trees and trim the branches?" He gave me a vague look and replied: "Yes, I want someone for the maintenance of my garden, but I prefer a man and not a child." I turned to call my father and uncle and they came running one after the other. The owner opened the gate, and we entered to the garden.

"I think this garden needs around three days of hard work, don't worry about your pay. I will make you happy," he said.

He led us to an old shed in the yard. As he opened the aluminum door, a musty smell filled our noses. It seemed as if it had been neglected for years. My uncle moved with unwonted alacrity, as if revived by this chance to earn a living. He emerged with an old shovel and tiller mattock. He gave the shovel to my father, lifted the tiller mattock, and placed it on his shoulder.

My father and uncle entered the garden, and I followed with the owner. As soon as they reached the first tree in the garden, my uncle inserted the tiller mattock in the ground to see what it could do. My uncle began digging the ground and clearing the weedy bushes around the tree, as my father shoveled dirt around the tree's trunk, preparing it for watering. The owner seemed reassured. He returned to his home with a smile on his face. Then I took the shovel from my father's hand and spelled him. After a quick rest, my father resumed digging. Then, I took the tiller mattock from my uncle's hand, in turn, and the three of us found our working rhythm.

We worked steadily until the seventh tree; then we took a rest in the shade. My father and my uncle looked at me as if we were all victorious in a fateful battle. In a single voice, they said: "Praise be to *Allah*, you have grown up." We lay stretched out under branches bowed by heavy clusters of quinces. From our garden repose, we pictured the future. Each of us imagined what he wanted. I saw myself taking my turn in helping my family, supporting my refugee mother, father and uncle. They saw in me a hope or a blessing coming from the remote corner of the garden. This hope promised them a new garden home overlooking a crystalline river.

After a time, my uncle broke the silence: "I want to eat. I am starving, and I cannot bear the hunger any longer." My father made a quick move and scooped up several apples. We ate apples until our stomachs were full. It looked like each of us had three bellies. When we were nourished, we started talking about our strange day. One of us mentioned mother, reminding us that she had lost her job, so we hastened to pick more fruit from the tree branches.

We put the gathered fruits in a cloth bag that my father had made for such an occasion and headed to our house in old Nazareth. After only a few strides, we felt someone just behind us, then heard a scream. We looked back to see the owner of the house carrying the orange peels and the remaining apples and pears. He cried out: "This is what I feared. You ruined my house. You ate my best fruit. My maid was right. I should have kicked you out as I did to the other beggars." He ran behind us, shouting profanities at our parents and our parents' parents, and he grabbed the bag of fruit from my father's neck. He banished us from his paradise on earth.

4

The Hyena of Sartaba

I was five years old or a little less when my father returned sad and tired from his job in Haifa. My mother asked him what was wrong. He answered: "I argued with my boss, Abu Daoud, today." He added that he was now unemployed. The minutes went by slowly and heavily in our household. What can children of a displaced family from Sirin do? Each one of our faces darkened in turn, father's, mother's, uncle Awad's, and mine. We were in a bind. Even when my father was working, we could barely cover rent and basic necessities. It was like we were back in the refugee days of 1948 when we squatted on the ground next to a restaurant in the center of Nazareth waiting for a miracle that might not happen.

In the mid-sixties, my father traveled to Haifa and stood as many other refugees did in *Al-Hanatir* square waiting for someone to hire him. One day, a Jewish contractor named Abu Daoud arrived looking for workers. He approached my father and asked: "Would you like to work on a daily basis?" My father nodded yes, and moments later he was in the bed of a truck with two other workers, one from the Sandala village, the other from al-Muqaible. They stopped at a broken-down house in Haifa and immediately started on the hard work of taking it apart and hauling its stones to a new location. My father, who was in his fifties then, filled the rubber bucket with dirt and building material from the demolished house and emptied it in the bed of the truck. One fateful day, he quarreled with his boss who fired him and forced him to leave. He went back to our home in Nazareth dragging the heels of disappointment.

Naji Dhaher, "The Hyena of Sartaba," trans. Hazza Abu Rabia. Translated with permission by Naji Dhaher.

As the hours dragged on, we understood our true status as sons of a displaced family. Sleep was impossible. We sat in silence, each of us consumed by our predicament, wondering what we could do next. How would we pay the rent? The days were passing so quickly and another payment would be due soon. If we were late on the rent, even two or three days late, the landlord would come to our door and shout: "If you don't have any money, you can't stay in the house!" My poor mother would beg him to wait until my father got paid and promise to pay him the rent in person. But we had used up our chances. The end of the month was fast approaching, and eviction loomed.

"What a hardship this is," my mother said to my dad. I heard my father calming her, saying, "May God help us." My mother replied: "How will he help us? I stopped working, and tomorrow we will not find bread on our table."

Moments passed and our spirits shrank. My father, mother, and uncle were thinking of a solution. I was also thinking. I looked much older than I was, and I spoke wisely which made my mother say that I was an old man. She did not hesitate to draw the neighbors' attention towards me: "The old man has entered the house," she would say. She warned, "Beware of what you say in front of him. Otherwise, he might spread whatever he hears from you all the way to Mount *Sartaba's* trees, and he may cause all of you a scandal we can avoid."

The atmosphere at home was heavy with concern for tomorrow. Our problem seemed insolvable until my father broke the silence with surprising news: "Tomorrow I will start to sell Araqsous (licorice root drink) in the market."

"Where will you get it from?" My mother replied.

My father said: "I will go to the forest of *Sartaba* tonight with my shovel and extract what is necessary. If God protects us tonight and we have the roots of licorice, we will make a drink that people like to buy. We'll price it so it sells, and we'll make money."

My mother thought for a moment and replied: "Your idea could work, but don't you fear the ghoul of *Sartaba*?"

My dad reassured her: "He is more merciful than human monsters. I cannot allow our situation to deteriorate more than it already has."

"Will you do this alone?" my mother asked him.

He replied, "No, I will take your brother A'wad. It is enough that we tolerated him unemployed until he reached forty years. Surely, he can help me." After a few moments, he added, "I will take our little boy with us, too."

Then my mother leaned on her bed, "Leave our son alone, he is still very young and he cannot bear such hardships. If the ghoul of *Sartaba* appears, what will you do?"

I stood by the door, listening, and saw my father stand up and reply, "Listen my dear. It is true that our son is still very little. Yet, he should know how difficult his life will be from now on. Don't you want him to become a strong man who can face hardships?"

My mother paused, then said, "But he is still so young ..."

My father seemed not to hear my mother's words. I knew he had carried the point when I saw him put on his British military pants. Thankful for any way out of our mess, Uncle A'wad rose quickly, opened the broken closet door and found his own British military pants. In a few minutes the two looked like first-class British horsemen. I surprised everyone, especially my mother, by putting on my British pants as well. My father bought these pants for me from the thrift market in Haifa. Within seconds, we looked like a mini-battalion preparing for a big battle. Still trying to dissuade me, my mother ran behind me and asked: "Where are you going tonight, my sweetheart?" I told her what I knew she expected to hear: "I cannot leave my father and my uncle alone tonight. I must join them." I reassured my mother that I was nearly a man.

My mother finally relented. She stood motionless and followed us with her eyes until we were out of sight. The night was covering its creatures while we were on our way to *Sartaba*. I embarked on this journey with my father and my uncle full of ambition to contribute even a small part to the battle of existence, our existence. I did not turn my face back because I was sure that my mother's tears were falling, and seeing her pain would have weakened me and ended my journey to manhood before it began. I did not want to be like the other small boys standing aside, watching his family suffer, powerless to help.

The three of us left a difficult night behind, and headed toward the more difficult night that awaited us in *Sartaba*. We moved from squares to streets and from valley to highland. The three of us were afraid, and without the hope of a better future we wouldn't have continued. Our eyes moved in all directions, to the trees that were lying in the dark, and to the houses far behind us. If one of us stretched out his hand in the dark he could barely see it. It seemed that our fear frightened an owl in a tree. It cried out loudly and each of us froze in his place.

"There is no other way back," my father said. "We must go into the depths of the forest where there is a great old tree with roots of licorice. We will search for it with our hands until we find it." Then he lifted his arms and said: "O Lord, we ask you to help us accomplish our mission. We do not want to be rich, but we need something simple to help manage our lives." Uncle A'wad asked my father: "Do you think that we will be able to gather all that we need to sell the licorice drink tomorrow?" My father responded: "We must make the necessary effort. But if it takes all night or longer, we'll stay. Hurry now, move fast, there is no time to waste."

As my dad pronounced these words, I saw a shape move through the nearby thicket. I froze with fear. My father told me not to be afraid. We were near the heart of *Sartaba*. Indeed, moments later, we stood beneath the fabled tree in the center of the forest. My father sat on the ground, indifferent to his surroundings, concentrating only on gathering what he needed from the roots of the licorice. He asked me and my uncle to collect dried branches that would burn easily. He added, "The hyena will not approach a burning fire." After a few moments, my uncle and I had gathered enough wood, and my father put a Nobles cigarette in his mouth and lit it; then he pressed on the lighter and quickly the pile of wood caught fire and the flames rose under the high branches. The darkness turned to half day. My father asked us to smother the fire a little so that the forest would not burn. Each of us took a heavy stick including my father, and we tried to beat back the flames by striking the fire three times followed by another three strikes. We finally had the fire under control. At that moment, everything in front of us became clear. My father extended his hands to the ground and started to dig. My uncle and I joined him. "Three hands are not like one hand," said my father. He continued to cheer me up. "Early tomorrow morning we will be in the garage area in Nazareth. We will be shouting and selling licorice drink. We will be swarmed by the workers who head to Haifa like flies on candy. As I told you, we will set a reasonable price, and we will sell everything we make and make a lot of money. Let's move quickly my darling, don't stop now."

My father's words reassured me a bit, but my hysterical fear of hyenas, especially the hyena of *Sartaba*, was not so easily contained. His eyes shined in the dark and rekindled the fear that had been dormant in my bones since I had first been aware of the world. I had heard stories of this hyena ever since my family was displaced. He ate a knight who was on his way from Dabouryeh village to Nazareth. He attacked him in the night by spraying him with his urine from his tail until the knight was subdued. The dazed knight became a delicious meal for the hyena. In another incident, the feet of a hungry hyena brought it to a soldier who was sleeping under a tree in the plain of Dabouryeh. He approached the soldier and dazed him with his urine as he did the knight, and he devoured him leaving behind only a piece of the soldier's leg and his boots. It was said that the hyena returned the next night and ate those too. Whenever I heard such tales, I felt an inconceivably intense fear. I often dreamt of the hyena stalking me in the cold winter nights. When I felt him open his mouth to chew my bones, a strong force of unknown origin suddenly filled me, and I took a lighter to a shroud to repel that hungry hyena with fire. The hyena then began to groan and run away. My fear broke and speech returned to my throat. I woke up from my nightmare, and I would wake up my mother as well, and she would read verses from the Qur'an to stop the evil. Then I would go to sleep despite my fear, but my fear would return to wake me up again, and I would lie in bed thinking of the hyena of *Sartaba*.

The three of us worked furiously as if our lives depended on our digging, and we were surprised to see the hyena approach emboldened by the weakening flames. I stuck to my father's back, terrified. My father hugged me and said, "Don't worry my young son, I am with you." Then he directed his words to my uncle and said, "It seems that our curse took the shape of a ferocious hyena. God protect us tonight from him and from the scourge that he may bring to us."

My uncle did not answer. He was too busy gathering more firewood. My father began assiduously gathering wood as well. It seems that Abu el-Hassan, the hyena, took advantage of this opportunity. When my father was away from the fire, he sprayed him with his urine. My father trembled in his place and was about to fall to the forest floor. We rushed to his aid and offered him water. Then we dragged him to the great tree still clutching the dry wood he had collected, and the new wood sent the flames high again. We had no choice but to continue digging if we hoped to reach our goal before dawn.

We were calm for a short time, but this tranquility was replaced by terror when the hyena appeared again. His eyes glistened with a rapacious lust for human flesh, our flesh. My father said: "It seemed like he would not leave us tonight. He was hungry, very hungry. When the hyena starves, he will forget his fear and will attack anything that comes his way. That's what my brothers from Muqaibla and Sandala village who work with me told me." My friend Abu Daoud added: "When the hyena starves, he forgets the Lord of his creation, and he attacks."

The faster we dug, the more that accursed creature threatened us. In the end, my father had no choice but to make the most difficult decision of his life. He said to Uncle A'wad: "This hyena will not leave us alone, he will prey upon us all."

"What do you mean?" my uncle replied shivering with horror. My father told him: "I understand what is going on. If the situation remains the same, the hyena will devour us, and we will never return to our home. I have thought it through. We have only one option. If it goes right, we will get back to our house safely. Tomorrow we will sell licorice root drink. Yet if I fail, I ask you to forgive me and to take care of the family. Take care of your younger sister and her baby. We have only one option. One of us must sacrifice himself for the others."

My father put his hand on my uncle's mouth and started to take off his clothes. Within moments, my father stood naked as his Lord created him. There he was, my father, a naked man in the middle of the forest. Before my uncle and I could speak, my father was advancing toward the hyena. He walked with a steady pace. He had the footsteps of someone who was trying to convince the hyena to give up on his meal. My father stood facing the hyena and the shadow he cast was huge.

Did my father make the hyena change his mind? Maybe, I don't know. My father looked straight in the eyes of that fierce hungry hyena, and I listened to him as if he were talking to him saying: "Take it easy, Abu el-Hassan. Take it easy, brother. When you are hungry, be nice to me. May God reward you with ample prey in this forest. Let me continue my journey with my loved ones. My enemies' guns missed me,

Abu el-Hassan, and you want to chew me with your sharp teeth? I pray to God to have mercy on me. Do you think that we can be friends from this night onwards? Come my love. Does my humanity intercede for me here? Come here and sleep."

My father patted the hyena's head, while the hyena kept quiet. Before we could feel relieved by this momentary detente, the hyena sprayed my father with his intoxicating urine. In an instant, the monster had disappeared among the trees. In a trance, my father followed, having forgotten all he ever knew of loving humanity and the fabled tree.

My father followed behind the hyena of *Sartaba*, and I stayed by the fire with my uncle. Where did my father go? Would he be able to reconcile with the hyena as our ancestors did? This question filled our minds, but we found no answer.

It was midnight or later, and the darkness of the forest surrounded us. After a short absence, the hyena returned to the fabled tree. However, we were prepared with heaps of dry wood. We stoked our fire at intervals and continued digging. Our pile of roots was growing, but it was not big enough. We must continue. After an hour or two, dawn would arrive. Then we would carry what we had back home, prepare our drink, and set out for the garage area of Haifa, where the workers gather.

My uncle asked me: "Do you think we should leave now? We have enough roots. I know you understand my words well. As for your father, if he is alive, he will follow us, and if ..."

I put my hand on my uncle's mouth and added: "Please do not say it. Stay silent. I do not want to hear bad news about my father. My father always wished to return to Sirin, and I always hoped that he would one day get his wish."

After a moment of silence, my uncle asked again, "Do you think we should leave now and come back tomorrow?"

But his mind was already made up. Before I could answer, he told me to walk in front of him towards the house. No sooner had we left the fire than the hyena launched another attack, this time in a way I had never imagined, not even in my nightmares. My tongue was tied and my saliva was dry. My uncle was also terrified, but he made himself strong so that he and I would not collapse. He didn't want to give the hyena the opportunity to finish the two of us. We turned back to the tree and put the roots on the ground, then we added more wood to the fire, and stuck to each other for protection.

We had to endure this harsh and difficult night, or we would all be destroyed. The hyena circled us; we were surrounded and only a miracle could save us. It was clear to us both that we faced an absurd fate and the only way to survive was to have patience.

The hyena circled closer as if he were determined to have his meal before the last remnants of darkness had faded into dawn. The more he circled, the fiercer he became. All the while, our fear and terror were also growing. My uncle raised his hands through the darkness and spoke from the depths of his desire for life, "The dawn will come in one hour, and this ruthless animal will be gone. O heaven, Give us one hour of relief!" But the sky did not respond to my uncle's request, and the darkness of our harsh night covered the forest and the sleeping creatures. Abu el-Hassan circled as if he didn't want to give up the spoils that were so close, yet not quite in reach.

Ah, Abu el-Hassan. Why do you become more brutal as the end of the night approaches and the light of the day gets closer?

At once, my uncle seemed to lose his strength. Desperate to live, he whispered in my ear, "I know now that he will not leave us on his own. He is determined to finish us before the day begins. We must do something."

I asked him, "What can we do? He is closing in."

My uncle scratched his head and asked, "You heard your father when he told me to take care of you and my sister, your mother?"

I replied, "Yes, I heard him."

Then my uncle said in a voice that I will not forget for all my life, "I will try to distract him just as your father did with his rare courage."

I yelled at my uncle, "You want to sacrifice yourself as a meal for the hyena?"

My uncle looked straight into my eyes and said, "We only have this possibility, otherwise we will both be eaten. You must live. Do you understand the meaning of these words? You must live and carry our message. You must live. Do you understand?"

He started to do exactly as my father did. My uncle removed his clothes and walked towards the hyena. The view was terrible. My uncle was approaching the hyena naked while the hyena was moving his head waiting for him to get closer. My uncle continued to get closer and closer to him. When he reached the standing hyena, he extended his hand to pet its cheek.

"Hello Abu el-Hassan, my beloved. I am coming to you on my own. I want to have peace with you. Where did you take my sister's husband? In what mound have you hidden him?" My uncle spoke such sad words, but his face showed signs of hope. My uncle addressed Abu Hassan with a tenderness that was not strange to him. The hyena listened to him as if he understood what he was saying. The decisive moment had arrived. The hyena circled my uncle several times and urinated from his tail, spraying my uncle's nose. My uncle seemed to lose control of himself. The hyena disappeared into the forest, and my uncle followed behind him.

Only when the night was over did I realize that a new life was conferred on me by my father and my uncle.

The dawn appeared on the horizon. I took the root pack and set off for home with the feeling that I had just suffered a terrible loss and had received my life back at the same time.

5

The Departure

The departure of my mother Zarifa on February 20, 2007, followed by the death of my brother Jawhar and my uncle's wife Khadra in the same year, took me back to the greatest departure in my life. This was the day of my father's departure in 1975, thirty-one years ago. One morning my mother came to wake me. This, in itself, was unusual. Her tone was urgent, and I lifted my head with fear and concern. I realized with all my senses that something momentous had happened in my life. My mother left my room and I followed her to find my father lying on the floor. I called my late brother from his room, and we carried my father's body to his bed.

We took the necessary steps to bid farewell to my father. May God have mercy on him. I went to the cemetery of Nazareth in the city center and asked the cemetery keeper what I must do to bury my father. He asked me if we were originally from Nazareth. I said no and added that my family came to Nazareth in the year of the Nakba. The cemetery guard told me if that is the case, I could go to the "strangers' cemetery" in the western part of the city. There, we buried my father under a pine tree, away from his village Sirin, his beloved home, where he deeply wished to be buried.

When my family ended up in Nazareth, after their exile journey during the Nakba years, my father, who was in his fifties, spoke to me and my other brothers and relatives about how he witnessed with his own eyes the occupation of his village, how he became homeless and poor after being a landlord, how he had been forced to live a difficult life. He went to Haifa after he obtained a permit from the Israeli military rulers, who controlled the lives of the remaining Palestinians

Naji Dhaher, "The Departure," trans. Hazza Abu Rabia. Translated with permission by Naji Dhaher.

inside the newborn state. The government permit allowed him to travel to a designated area, but only for work. He found a job with a Jewish employer, Abu Daoud, who hired Palestinian workers to fill the bed of his truck with dirt. Abu Daoud would haul the dirt to another location, dump it, and return for the workers to fill his truck again and again.

My father shoveled dirt for more than twenty years. Every Friday, he returned to Nazareth, a tired old man, exhausted by a life of displacement from his hometown Sirin. What added to his suffering was that he worked like a slave in the new Jewish buildings of Haifa.

My father and other workers suffered the fate of the ancient Greek legend Sisyphus, who was doomed to roll the same boulder up the same mountain every day. My father accepted his work and his new reality. He realized that this was his fate and that he had to endure it until the end. He would only complain to God. He always considered any other complaint a humiliation.

The sustenance my father brought home each week from Haifa was always accompanied by an unspoken tension. During my childhood I felt that my father was a satisfied person. When he returned home once every week and sometimes once every two weeks, he deducted very little money from what he earned for cigarettes and for a little food. He used to give the rest to my mother. As I grew older, my sharp eyes saw the deep sadness behind his satisfaction.

My father's heart was accustomed to this sadness, but he accepted his fate with patience. He knew how to deal with his loss. He often told me and others that the lands he owned must one day be returned to him. He remembered the name of each part of that land as if it were his own. He would recite the names of the most fertile plots: *Al-Rabidah, Al-Jabshinah,* and *Al-Qusaybah.*

Despite his love for his village and everything related to it, my father only visited it once, or perhaps twice, after being exiled. The first time was after the war of 1967 when a number of family members came from the city of Irbid in Jordan and asked us to accompany them to our village. My brother Jawhar, who was a baker in a bakery owned by a man named Al-Shamoot, said that he would rent a taxi and we would go to the village. And that's what happened.

Each of us, father and his relatives, and my family, took a seat in the car, and I recalled that each of them was like an infatuated lover.

The nearer we came to the village, the faster our hearts beat. Our eyes flashed and Uncle Mustafa said, "Hello, childhood fields." They were addressing the empty spaces in their village, but these empty spaces were filling their souls. They yearned for their village, as a husband yearns for his beloved wife after a long absence. Oh, our beloved land how much we are yearning for you, and how much the longing for you has killed us.

Finally, we arrived at the village. Each of us looked among the scattered stones for what had once been the family home. We all cried in our own way, some without showing tears, some so overcome that their tears watered the land.

In my youthful days, my dreams were not bounded by limits. I looked at the far horizon and told myself that someday I would get there, and my soul would extend from space to space. I just needed to find a place where life could start, and that was an old house, half of it sinking in the ground. Once I looked inside it, I saw my mother represented by the remains of a skeleton. I left in search of the village cemetery. When I looked for the graves of my grandfather and grandmother, I saw nothing but the emptiness. Suddenly I felt two bradawls stabbing my back. Would I be another victim? Was this the end? Were those who raped the village and took her soul, returning to continue their mission? O God, what cruelty was this? I slowly turned to see my attacker, as if moving deliberately could postpone my fate, and my eyes crossed his eyes. It was my father. I read in his eyes a message that I would never forget no matter how many days and nights pass. His message was a simple question: Will I be buried in this beloved land or in a strange place?

Years later, when my father passed, he was buried in a strange land, in the strangers' cemetery. Not many people attended the funeral, and very few extended their condolences.

My father is gone, but his restlessness remains. Although we buried him, he haunts this strange land, a restive witness to the pain that still breaks our hearts.

6

The Meow of the Mountain

As I stepped off the bus near the port, my ears were filled with a cat's meowing. The cat sounded sad, which made me forget the purpose of my trip from the town of Nazareth to the city of Haifa. I was visiting my sister, who lives deep in old Haifa. I walked hastily because I wanted to tell her about a robbery that shook my soul. I have nothing left in this life other than a loving sister who has lived in Haifa with her husband and children for more than thirty years.

When her husband, who is a son of Haifa, proposed many years ago, I opposed the marriage. I told her that I don't like to travel, so I would only be able to visit her on special occasions and holidays. In the early periods of her life there, I visited often. Over time, however, my visits became more and more sporadic, and they have stopped almost entirely in recent years. But I have returned today because I must share my misfortune with someone who cares. I will tell my sister that I saved up money to end our family's homelessness, which began the year of the Nakba, when my parents had to leave their village, Sirin. I will tell her that I saved enough money and hid it among my papers and books. I will lay my tired body over there on a couch near her to unwind. I will hold my head in my two hands, and she will ask what happened to me. Then, I will start to cry, and I will forget that I am in my fifties. I am going to tell her with sorrowful eyes shedding tears that they stole the money I saved to buy a house, and I will need another fifty years to save enough money to buy a house and settle down as I have dreamed of all my years. Just as I was about to live my dream, it escaped like the wishes that slipped through my fingers when I wasn't looking. I had lived this visit in my mind for weeks, but on my way to Haifa, I was harassed by crazy

Naji Dhaher, "The Meow of the Mountain," trans. Hazza Abu Rabia. Translated with permission by Naji Dhaher.

thoughts. I began to wonder how my sister would receive me. Would she forgive me for forgetting her in a foreign land?

I walked steadily towards the old town, and the meowing followed me. This plaintive sound filled the streets. Everything in this town is meowing. My soul is meowing along with the trees, even the sails of the ships moored at the port of Haifa are meowing. I stopped walking to my sister's house in old Haifa. I made a knee-jerk decision to follow the meow. I must get to the bottom of it, even if the cost is a return trip to town with all my sorrows.

I ventured deep into the old town discreetly, led by the sad meow. As I got closer, I arrived at a mountain of discarded tires. I drew nearer. The meowing was loud in my ears. I felt that I had reached its very source. Surely, I have journeyed to the source of secrets, to the depths of that weeping meow.

I peered into the mountain of scrap tires. I spotted a dark head moving slowly and listened carefully; the mewing was not far off. With all my senses, I plumbed the depth of the meow. Then, I saw her, a single cat. Surely her parents left her all alone here, and she was crying for her wretched luck in this life. Who is this cat? Could she have been displaced during the year of the Nakba, and was she not stranded here alone shedding hopeless tears? Couldn't she have found some solution to the long humiliation of her displacement? When she found her dream house, she went there to live in peace and dignity, but she was turned out and lost her way and never found it again. I shared a sympathetic glance with that little cat. But I am homeless, too. So what could I do? What could I do for her while I was only a stranger in this friendless city?

I sat on an odd-sized old tire, which was lying far away from his brothers in the mountain. I made it my seat. The cat's meow was getting fainter and fainter, deep in the mountain. But it reached deep down inside me, and from the darkness of the tire pile, the cat's eyes met mine directly. I could not leave her in this dreary mountain alone and sad. I would take her with me. Where would I take her while I also do not have a home? I would take her, and I meant it. I could not leave her to unkind fate. I could not leave her alone like this. I resolved to take her.

I suddenly stood up and strained my fist, grinding what were left of my teeth. I made my eyelids small and opened them wide. I ran towards the wild mountain. I attacked it with all my pent-up frustration. Where did that little cat disappear to? Finding no trace of her, I took a more methodical approach, carefully removing the tires one by one. Where did that little cat disappear to? I took the mountain apart and built it up again a small distance away. But I could not find that cat. She was gone, as if she was swallowed by the earth. She ceased to exist. Was I hallucinating? Where did that little cat disappear to? The meowing stopped for a moment and then filled old Haifa again. I headed to my sister's house in the depths of Haifa city. I walked slowly, distracted by this mystery, when a strange thought struck me, and I began to run towards my sister's house. I ran and ran and ran, and the meow came after me, so I ran faster and faster, thinking: Who knows that I might find my poor sad cat there at my sister's house, perhaps on her lap?

7

Displaced, Son of a Displaced

He tried to get some rest, but it was futile. The image of his daughter, his beloved baby, disturbed him and he could get no sleep. All his attempts were wasted, but in the past, he knew how to find rest. That is right, in the past when he attempted to bring drowsiness, he needed some effort, but he could always find rest. But on this gloomy night, following a day as bitter as colocynth leaves, sleep eluded him. His wife, his life's companion, had pulled the carpet from under his feet, and he found himself far from his loved ones. His torment was complete when she sent his young daughter away from what once was their home, but was hers, alone, today!

He stared blankly at the reception room. He had been sleeping in this room since he found himself displaced and lonely; he, his books and his computer have occupied this old, remote apartment. When she refused to spend her life with him, he abandoned the home of his happier days, where he slept alongside his wife. He could not stand to imagine the boys' beds empty, so he avoided thinking about that room as well. He had become a stranger to his own house.

He felt suffocated, as if someone were grabbing him by the throat. What was going on with him? Was this just a long nightmare from which he would awake to his old life with his family? His feelings led him to the window overlooking the garden. He saw only silent darkness. He looked more carefully to see if anything was moving in the heart of the night. He waited for a long time, but nothing moved. The five years that had passed since he was forced out of his house taught him that the night was a senseless beast and the light that he was waiting for would not come.

Naji Dhaher, "A Displaced Father's Displaced Son," trans. Hazza Abu Rabia. Translated with permission by Naji Dhaher.

He returned to bed. What could he do? What he faced was beyond his powers. In the distant past, on the day he came from the Safafreh neighborhood to Nazareth Illit, he felt like something big would happen. He harbored strange fears for his five-year-old son—a crazy person may kidnap him or a passing car may run him over. And he never overcame his fears for his young daughter, who brightened his world with her laughter. Then years later, he discovered that his fear was misdirected; he should have noticed that the danger would come from a seemingly safe place. He was not expecting even in his worst imagination that the fear would sweep him from his beloved wife's door after three decades. But that's what happened. He is now, on this long night, hoping to forget the past, he wants to remember nothing at all. The long destruction of the Nakba and his terrible personal loss are in the past. In front of him is a future of constant vigilance—the next blow could destroy his tired heart and send him back to the darkness from which he came.

"No, that will not be," he said while trying to force open the iron bars of the window. No that will not be. He would escape as close to unscathed as possible. His successive losses taught him that courage was the patience of an hour, and those who bear the most would be chosen in the kingdom of hope. But how to bear what he just learned this morning, that his beloved little daughter lives with her sister, after her mother kicked her out of her house? How could he be patient? He did not know what to do. This was the last thing he expected to hear from his eldest daughter this morning. How could he be patient? The question troubled him, and he prepared himself for a new Nakba.

He asked, "What happened to your sister?" His eldest daughter said, "I thought you knew that mom kicked her out of the house. She's been at my house for two days." When he finally started breathing again, he put the phone back in its place and pondered how he could bring his daughter back home. There was no easy solution. Since he was not at home and could not get close to home without his ex-companion calling the police, he would need to involve a relative, but who would do this for me? Of all his extended family, the one survivor was feeble. Shall I go to him? Yes, let's do it, what am I waiting for? A drowning man cannot wait to grasp a lifeline. That's how he found himself rushing in the evening hours towards his last relative's home. The way was long. He held no illusions: Either no one would help him, and he would be drowning in his darkness forever, or a miracle would ensue in an age that did not know miracles. He did not want to go, but pushed himself to walk quickly. At last, he arrived, stopped at the door of a closed house, and felt himself drowning in the darkness. He was suddenly unsure. "No, I won't knock on this door, I have knocked on this door more than once in the past and it has never opened." He stood alone in the darkness. "Shall I knock on the door one more time and add another defeat to my notebook of losses? Let it be. Yes, let's add another defeat. It could not harm me further."

He approached the door and raised his hand to knock on the door, but he felt a sudden weakness. He very slowly lowered his hand and walked back into the darkness, looking for another door. But every door he tried was locked. Where could he go? Where now? He kept walking: seven steps, ten steps, a full thousand, thousands more until he reached the door of his own house. He fished his key out of his pocket and opened his door, the only door that would open for him. All other doors were closed. "Everyone is busy with their own lives, and you should die in your sadness and sorrow," he said to himself as he shut his apartment door and trudged to his bed in the reception room to lay his body down and wait for the sleep that had deserted him over five years ago at the time of his second eviction.

***

He lifted his body from his bed in the reception room. He felt heavy. But he renounced what he felt. He headed back towards his old apartment door and out to the street. He had to do something. He could not accept such a situation, and it was clear to him that he had two choices: Either live a lovely life and make your friends rejoice or suffer an untimely death and peeve your enemies. He could not accept a total loss. He thought to himself, "There is still time to maneuver, even to adventure," and this thought propelled him on his way faster than the sword cuts the air. The road ahead of him was endless and he was running without fear of the darkness before him. He would do anything to bring his beloved daughter back to her home. He ran and ran with the night by his side.

8

Woman of Love

Dear Sawalef,

Your break-up with me and departure from my beloved city have left me bewildered. Even as I write, I never imagined the day would come when I would impose such a request. You are the crowned queen among all the queens of our precious town—the one all the Palestinian lovers would die for.

What forced you to leave this place, my precious? Is it the times? Or the routine? Or the dream of far horizons? Or the most beautiful horizon, as you have repeated more than once? After your request, I have been obsessively reviewing our past, our love, and our city to find the source of the plague that aggrieves us lovers and our sweet home.

I sat down with my friends in the city of boredom, our old city, and we plotted a way out of this deadening dullness. We sat silent for a long time before we departed without a plan. Days later, we sat down together once more, but still nothing.

By our third meeting, we felt trapped in a prison of boredom and loneliness. No one spoke. Words seemed powerless against the prison walls of our lives until our silence had become so oppressive that each of us, as if by instinct, turned his eyes to the green horizon in the distance. I was the first to see his white horse standing there and waiting for someone who would escape the oppressive silence that surrounds us. Very quickly, the horse surprised my friends, and before my astonishment could settle in, my imagination took me back to my childhood in our displaced village, Sirin. There, I saw a picture featuring you, my childhood friend and lover. I connected the dots and dazzled my friends with my sudden decision to fly with my white horse to where you stay,

Naji Dhaher, "Woman of Love," trans. Hazza Abu Rabia. Translated with permission by Naji Dhaher.

to the world of magic and beauty, prepared, at last, to play my special role in our history.

I shared my plan with hundreds of refugee friends from the displaced villages of our country. They merely smiled as I had smiled earlier, as if we were complicit in this thing. We all rushed to our horses in the open space. We chased them a bit as they ran in front of us, but every person reached his own horse in his own way. When we rode our horses, we felt light and free. What a wonderful moment to see the white horse, my horse, beside other Arabian horses! The picture was nearly realized. Nothing was missing except what you and I had imagined together with our kindred feelings that brought us back to the tenderness of Mother Nature.

To make this long story short, each person rode his horse to his displaced village, and I found myself alone riding towards the village of my dreams where I left you, a young girl. I rode past all the soldiers, tanks, and planes. I left these obstacles behind, one by one. As I approached our village, a flame of light that sprung from the bottomless dark led the way until I realized that the light of my journey was your glorious face. What a beautiful thing for one to meet his own past! What a beautiful thing for my past to grow up just as we've grown up. You were so beautiful then, when I first left you. We did not need to know each other back then. You departed from my memory, and I departed from yours. The time between us had long been covered with dust. Yet across lost time I extended my hand to you, and you gave yours to me. I flew to you like a bird over the mountains. I flew towards my country mountains, along with the rest of the horses carrying the other knights and their loved ones. We flew, flew, and flew together in one direction. We flew to the town of magic and beauty.

My dear Sawalef:
There, on fertile green land, surrounded by hills, where the Arabian horses wander, we built an unbelieveable home. I want to stop talking right here because there is nothing to add to what I have said in my earlier message with the exception that every moment I see you as a newly reborn woman, a woman who has a thousand faces and colors. A woman of an eternal love. I am directing this message to you, dear Sawalef. I hope that you will rethink your decision. I would like to remind you that

what brings us together is much more than what separates us. Come back to me! Come back to my friends, return to the city of magic and beauty! Come back to revive the city's soul once again. Come back to resurrect our love.

9

Accused on the Beach

I did not trespass on a restricted area, your Honor. Despite my accuser's claim, I did not violate it by air or by sea. All I did was pity a poor balbout fish and attempt to release him back into the water. You should be asking me now where this balbout fish came from. Now, now, I will tell you in a little bit. I just want to make it clear, sir, that I did not catch the balbout fish. It is true that I did not know fishing in Lake Tiberias is forbidden. Yet, I would like to tell you that I am no fisherman. I have no fishing rod or fishing net. You can send an inspector to my house to make sure that I am telling you the truth. God is my witness.

Go easy on me, sir. I am a simple human being and I was displaced by the Nakba storm from the village of Sirin with my family. I have wandered every corner of this country. I was born in Nazareth, the town, which I love like my own parents.

Do not grumble, sir. Please hear me out, and maybe you will be convinced of my innocence. I swear to God that I deserve to be set free. Do you want me to be clear and direct? OK, fine, I will be all that you want, and I will answer all your questions. My story started with this miserable wretched balbout fish when I was lying on the sand at the lake shore one day.

I do not hide from you that I was, at that moment, looking at a fisherman who seemed to be one of our cousins, sons of Sarah. I remember that moment because I was scared. I tried to hide my eyes from him out of fear that he would bring trouble with the law. We eyed each other surreptitiously. Then he approached and offered me the balbout fish.

I took the balbout fish, which was fully alive, from his hand and I watched his cunning smile. If I had been more wary of his shady look,

Naji Dhaher, "Accused on the Beach," trans. Hazza Abu Rabia. Translated with permission by Naji Dhaher.

I would not be standing here in this dismal hall waiting for your justice in a case where I should have been the accuser, not the accused.

I will not drag on, sir. I know that your days are different than mine. You are always busier than me. I do not have a job, and I am free all the time. Believe me, if it were not for this case, I would be relaxing on that beach still. I will make my long story short. I took the balbout fish and rushed to my broken car. I wanted to take it to my town before the _khawaja_[1] could change his mind and backpedal on his present to me. I do not know why I did what I did, maybe because it was the first time that my hungry hands held a balbout fish.

You want me to be brief, sir? OK, I will be brief. I looked in the eyes of the balbout fish lying beside me on the front seat, and they were full of the very fear and distress that I know so well. I am the son of Nakba who is still wandering in its pathways. I extended my hand to him to assure him that I would be his friend because we had something in common. Then, the poor balbout moved his fins in pain. I told him: "Do not worry my little one, do not worry. Now I will solve your problem, and perhaps the world will have mercy on me, too, and help me return home." It seemed that the poor being did not understand anything, but deep down in my heart I felt that he understood me, so I found a rusty old aluminum can and filled it with water. By some miracle, the water stayed in it.

I carried the aluminum can back to the scared balbout. I looked in his eyes; his fear was growing. I tried to soothe him. He should not suffer because he does not oppress his poor brothers. I lifted him from the seat gently, as if I had been trying to rescue him all the days of my life, especially after my wife kicked me out of my house to live alone. I put the balbout in the water. Sir, I wish you could have seen me at that moment. I swear to God I felt like I was back in my parents' village Sirin. It is true that the rusty aluminum can was a tight fit, but the poor balbout opened his eyes as if he were thanking me. Yes, sir, he wanted to thank me as I will thank you after you recognize my innocence. You would like me to focus more, sir? I will. Say no more. I respect your order; it is my pleasure to comply.

---

1 Khawaja is a Persian word that means "master." It is also used in reference to a foreign person. It is used by Palestinians to describe the Israelis.

When I arrived at my house in Nazareth, my feelings were all over the place. What should I do with my dear guest? I could not answer this difficult question, so I called my wife. Uh, I called her, right, even though she had made it known that she could not put up with my voice. I could think of no one else to consult on the issue of my balbout. So I picked up the phone and told her everything in detail while she muttered to herself something like, "God grant me patience."

Finally, after she knew the story, I asked her what I should do with my fearful and perplexed guest. As always, she yelled at me and said: "You and your balbout are not my concern; smash him dead with a hammer and eat him. If you do not want him, give him to me and I will cut off his head and cook him myself." She hung up just like that. I visualized my hand bringing down a hammer on the head of that poor creature, and I felt as if my wife were hitting my head with a hammer. I decided on something that nobody would expect in this unhappy world, especially from an exiled father's exiled son like me. You would like to know my decision, sir? Be patient please. I will let you know in due time.

I had a plan, and it was time to make it happen. My old car could carry me from Nazareth to Tiberias. But would I go there alone? Especially with night beginning to fall. The time passed slowly as it once passed on an ancient Arab poet named al-Nabigha al-Dhubiyani. Do you know al-Nabigha al-Dhubiyani, sir? I squinted my eyes and formed a diabolical idea. I would call my wife, she used to love the sea; she would have killed her own father to see the moonlight dancing on the surface of the lake. That was when I killed every hesitation, how cruel the word "kill" is, and asked her politely to come with me to take the poor balbout to his watery home.

After a few minutes, I heard my wife summoning me from the street. She would not come into my house because she always said it was filthy. I rose to meet her. We got in my car, placed our guest in his can in the back, and headed for Tiberias.

We stopped the car over there on the beach. I looked in all directions. The clear weather spurred me to action. I ignored the very bright sign on the fence saying, "Access to this Beach Is Forbidden." That sign drew my wife's attention, and she warned me not to enter the beach. But I did not heed her warning. I thought I would need only a few moments. But what happened went against all my expectations. When I released the balbout into the water, a car appeared out of the blue. Two men sprung out—each with a gun pointed at my face. In short, the two men took tons of pictures of me and my car. They gathered all my information, and told me that I had just violated two rules: 1) entering a forbidden beach, and 2) fishing for balbout fish. They added that I must pay for my transgressions in court, so here I am in front of you, sir. I hope that you rule that I am innocent. I did not catch that balbout. I only wanted to release him back to the water. May God have mercy on me and take me back to my village, please.

What did you say, your honor. Guilty? I am guilty? You say that despite everything I have told you? Believe me, sir, the *khawaja* is the one who caught that balbout, not me … He was the one who did the fishing, not me. All I wanted was to return the home-sick balbout to his own waters after the *khawaja* captured him.

10

The Fire

1 ————————————————————————————————

Ismael was holding Sara tightly when the fire broke out in the forest of the Roshpina settlement near Kiryat Shmona. Smoke drifted over the farm, and the lovers noticed flames climbing into the sky on the other side of the forest.

Without exchanging a word, they stood still eyeing the horizon. Each recognized the fire as a personal catastrophe. Silence prevailed until Sara wondered aloud: "What will we do?"

An impassive expression covered Ismael's fear as the weight of his predicament settled on him. He was the only Arab in the settlement, and all eyes would now turn to him. He would be damned before he could speak, and his words would mean nothing. He stood to lose everything beautiful and dear to him. He imagined himself in prison suffering through long nights far from Sara, far from the settlement he loves. He loved its land, its birds and—despite the hatred—its people. He imagined that the days would always smile on him, but the catastrophe that he had always heard about on the news had come to his settlement. The fire had come for him and his beautiful dreams. Heavy moments passed. Sara gave him a look of endless entreaty and spoke anxiously and slowly, "What shall we do?"

Ismael shared Sara's horror. He knew that the long and mysterious road he followed to this settlement, where he became the only Arab who eats, drinks, loves and sleeps among its people, was different from the long and mysterious road that brought Sara and her family to this settlement to eat, drink, love, and sleep. He knew that the intersection of their two roads was a dangerous place and also the only place he

Naji Dhaher, "The Fire," trans. Hazza Abu Rabia. Translated with permission by Naji Dhaher.

wanted to be. The day he saw her for the first time, he could not imagine meeting her under a certain pine tree. It turns out that it was not impossible. When the unthinkable became real, questions more complex than he had ever imagined also became real.

The first time he met Sara was in the cowshed; soon after, he met her for a second, third, and fourth time. After the first meeting, they watched how the animals paired off. They watched them with a passion that arose as if from nowhere, as if from instinct or fate or another unfathomable source. The two soon found themselves joining their separate selves into one body and one soul. They did not think about the future. They thought only about themselves, about their bodies and their spirit. Each felt a deep desire to connect to the other forever. In the beginning, they met in the barn, right under the owner's eyes. When they had something to fear, they came here, close to the forest, to share their love. They felt complete, alone together, in a world apart. But then this unexpected fire at this unexpected time dragged them back to the divided world.

If Sara asked Ismael a thousand times "What are we going to do?" he would still have had no answer. He was thinking about himself and he was thinking about her. He already considered himself the accused. Fate had brought them together, and if they remained together, she would be accused as well. Of course, he had a solid alibi. But to clear his name would mean to insist that Sara was alone with him at the other end of the forest! How could he admit this? More importantly, how could she admit this? Could he deliver her to the unknown? Sara could not bring herself to ask for Ismael's sacrifice. But she struggled with the thought of sacrificing herself. Everything in Sara was telling him don't speak our love, don't destroy me. Yet everything in her was also assuring Ismael: I want you to be safe. The lovers remained silent. Finally, Ismael took Sara's hand and led her back to the settlement. The flames climbed higher and higher on the other side of the forest.

2

The headlines in the evening papers read:
NEW FIRE BREAKS OUT IN *ROSHPINA* SETTLEMENT
COUNTRY ON FIRE
ALL SIGNS POINT TO ARAB ARONIST IN *ROSHPINA* FIRE
POLICE ON ALERT FOR ARSONIST
FIRE LIKELY RESULT OF PALESTINIAN UPRISING IN WEST
BANK AND GAZA

3

Ismael thought of fleeing the settlement more than once, but he knew that running would only confirm his guilt. When the police came and arrested him, as he knew they ultimately would, he saw that proving his innocence would cost Sara a terrible price. He imagined her religious family cutting her hair as is customary and imprisoning her in their house. The specter of this shame compelled Ismael to face his fate. After the inevitable happened, and he came before the investigators, he was told he would be considered "guilty until it is proven that you are innocent." In the beginning, they treated him well, but later they also used force. By design, they alternated between humane and brutal interrogation. Alone at night, he thought bitterly of the fate that led him down this mysterious road. He only ever wanted to live in peace, but the sons of bastards would not leave him alone. When he got to know Sara, he did not think that he was an Arab and that she was Jewish; he did not even think of himself as Palestinian. He was drawn to Sara, and she was drawn to him, human to human. They followed their insistent feelings to the cowshed, where they hugged for the first time. But it could have been anywhere in the world. Whenever they met they felt close to each other. Separated, now, he saw the bitter truth: She is Jewish from a conservative family and he is an Arab Palestinian, and every fire is his fire!

He could see the stars through the window of the detention room. He felt insurmountably alone, as if everyone in the world were asleep except for him. Before morning, he had decided to confess, and he did without hesitation. He described how he went to the forest and how he collected a pile of hay and set it on fire. The interrogator was over-joyed: "I knew that no one in the world burned the forest except you. Tomorrow you will stage the forest fire."

Now, in the interrogation room, he discovered that he was an Arab and that the interrogator was Jewish. Nevertheless, he kept wondering for the rest of the night if Sara was Jewish in this way too, but he did not reach a final answer.

The next day they gave him a matchbox to demonstrate how he set the fire. He did not hesitate and lit the forest again, for the first time.

The following day's headline read:

ARAB ARSONIST SETS ROSHPINA FOREST FIRE FOR SECOND TIME

> The police opened fire on an Arab while he was starting a fire. The suspect was wounded and transferred to an area hospital.

11

The Land of Terror

At the entrance of the mall, I saw them approaching. The little daughter let go of her father's hand and started running towards me. I had somehow forgotten how much I love her. The little girl was growing up. I held her tightly. Her father headed towards me and asked me to come along to the mall. He pointed to his daughter already in my arms and added: "She loves you, yet you have not visited for so long. She is always asking about you. Please be with us until she is satisfied with you and then go home." I told my son that I was happy to see him but that I am very busy and I have a lot of writing waiting for me. "I must return to my solitude," I said. "I will be sure to visit you later—soon, but now I cannot. My story cannot wait, and I must get it down before it leaves me."

The little girl caressed my moustache and said, "Grandpa I love you, I want to come with you." But come with me where? I am home only in the solitude of my silent room, with my delusional words and the unending madness of my writing. Home, to me, is an impenetrable wilderness, no place for my granddaughter. What shall I do? My son read the confusion in my eyes and said, "Father, take her for a short while and bring her back. Don't worry, she will soon get tired and want to come home." But how could I bring her back, my son? My son pointed to a small opening in the large fence that surrounded the mall to detain suspects in the event of a "suspicious object" or a "terrorist attack." He said, "You can sneak with her to the mall through this small opening."

My son and his wife grinned and walked off toward the mall entrance, leaving the little one around my neck. She asked "Where were you grandpa? I missed you." I smiled at her and said, "I am here now." I was about to tell her of my solitude, to tell her: "Your grandfather is

Naji Dhaher, "The Land of Terror," trans. Hazza Abu Rabia. Translated with permission by Naji Dhaher.

an old man, running behind his dreams." I thought better of it at the last minute, but she was persistent. The little girl wanted answers, and I tried to appease her. I will write you a story. She giggled and replied: "You are writing a story for me? Just tell it to me, instead! Recite it for me now! I like to listen to stories, but I do not like the stories my dad and mom tell me. They always repeat the same ones. I want to listen to a new story from you. So tell me a story!"

How I love this kid! I left her a while ago and I walked into my solitude, and now I am coming back to her after she filled my world with words. But I never thought she would learn to speak so quickly. Her dad, my son, did not say a word until he was much older than she is now. I still remember after he said his first words, I put my mouth to his ear and whispered, "How much I love you!" He hugged me, and said, "I love you, dad." From that day his blush disappeared, and his tongue spoke the sweetest words. But this kid, his little girl, she is asking me without fear to tell her a story. What a smart generation this is!

I walked away from the mall with the little one around my neck. Ever curious, she inquired, "Where are we headed? I want to go back. I want my mom and dad." Just like that, I understood that our special time was over for now. I turned to bring her back.

But the doors of the mall were now closed. The guard prevented me from entering: "Step back! You cannot go in." I asked him what happened. He shot me a knowing and malevolent look. I understood what his nasty look was telling me: *Your people are doing what you are doing and still you ask?*

I put the little girl down with vain hope that maybe he would relent at the sight of her. Perhaps he also has small kids. But he made a face. Apparently, he did not get the message.

I moved away and saw others outside the mall holding their babies in their arms; maybe they had loved ones inside like me. The soldiers blocked the entrance, keeping us out. But I remembered another way into the mall, an opening in the fence that my son pointed out. I walked toward the wall as inconspicuously as I could, then raised the little one with difficulty through the space cut into the fence. As soon as her small feet touched the land, she moved quickly as if she understood the circumstance: Without running her fastest she would not reach the mall or find her parents. I was trying awkwardly to follow her through when an armed soldier yelled to me: "Go back or ..." I got the message immediately; I did not need him to repeat it. We understand them quickly, but they do not understand us. For sixty years we've tried to convey our message, but they will not listen to us. Still, they expect us to understand each poisonous look.

I turned back as a feeling of helplessness overtook me. What has happened? I needed to know why the mall was suddenly locked. I peered through the glass doors. I tried to make out what happened, but all I saw was the same looped tape playing in my memory. I could picture the horror inside, though I could not see it. How could I know if my son and his wife were in there? How would I know that the little girl reunited with them safely? How miserable I would be if she were lost or her parents harmed. My mouth was dry. Was this the start of another brutal period? Would this day at the mall divide my life into another traumatic before and after?

Numbness entered my limbs: My son was in danger, his wife was in danger, my beloved little girl was in danger. What a moment! Why did God permit me to be born in this devastated country of anxiety and indignation? Why was I not born in a different country where birds flit through tree branches trailing songs behind them? Why was I born here, in this country, where the birds have stopped chirping and the sky has turned dark? What would I tell my son and his wife if they got out, now, in an hour or two, or after a day or two? What would I say to myself? I would say that I was stupid and just acted like someone who wants to write a story. What I would say would be petty compared to a father's and mother's tears. A grandfather who wants to be famous ...

Was the ultimate end approaching? Just maybe. I wished I had not passed near this damned mall. I wished I had stayed home in the wilderness of my solitude, away from this conflicted European society.

The moments passed slowly outside the mall. I stood alone in front of the cement blocks. I saw nothing but infinite sadness in a land of sand whose wretchedness has no limits. How happy I would be if I had stayed in today! I wish I had remained in my lonely, miserable world chasing after a runaway story. My solitude I can endure, but this I cannot. Now the cycle of pain is almost complete. Now I feel like a living palm tree in the Arabian Desert.

What could I do while the mall was closed and the soldiers guarded the doors with their merciless eyes? Should I do as the soldiers and the guards command? Yes, it is time to leave, for who am I to bend heavily armed soldiers to my wishes. Let me cave in to that moment and allow time to furnish the answers that I cannot provide myself. After all the beautiful stories I have written, my pen could not shield me from the Tomahawk missile in this soldier's eyes.

So let me turn my head into another block of cement.

After what seemed like hours of waiting in fear, not willing to leave, not willing to risk annoying the guards, I started to decompress. The image of my little girl appeared in my skies again. This vision spoke to me, "Grandpa, why did you stay away? Why did you leave me alone for so long amongst our enemies? Did your stories trick you, and did you chase after them?" A tear fell down my face. I did not know what I would tell her. And I still did not know what I could do except wait. When would I know? I may get the news tomorrow.

I closed my eyes because I did not want to see such a world. Let the world endure its nightmare, and let it confer on me the comfort of a dream. I opened my eyes and saw only soldiers and guards everywhere. I tried to yell: "Let me through! Let me in! I must be with my loved ones!" But my tongue was broken. I shut my eyes, then I opened them again. Oh my God, how terrifying this place is.

12

A Very Ordinary Scene

A notable journalist pressed the accelerator of his Cortina as he sped toward his Nazareth suburb after a day's work. On the dashboard, a picture of his wife looked at him sternly: "Don't you dare hurry. If you keep speeding, you'll regret it! If you keep speeding, I will throw myself out of the car, and you will be in big trouble for the rest of your life. You know what a woman is capable of doing in this country? The police are just waiting for a signal from a woman and a new chapter of your life will start."

Praise be to *Allah*, if his wife were with him, she would grill him as she did yesterday, when she threatened to go to the police, and in vain he tried to convince her that he was in the right, and he is not trying to disobey the police, because they were just waiting for an Arab to fall into their hands to avenge him. The thought made him shiver with apprehension. So he pleaded with his wife even though they had repeated this same quarrel for thirty years of marriage, and even though he knew she would not call the police.

No, his wife would not call the police. He stepped heavily on the accelerator. When he came to the junction on the edge of his neighborhood, he stopped. Seeing no cars, he again accelerated. When, at the last second, he saw a car approaching him, he pressed even harder on the gas as he always did on such occasions. Praise be to *Allah*, nothing happened, and he continued towards home.

A few cars were in the street; then, he noticed a speeding police car in his rear-view mirror. He thanked God again that he had made it safely through the junction and instinctively slowed down to let the police car pass. The police car sped toward him. He praised God once again and

Naji Dhaher, "A Very Ordinary Scene," trans. Hazza Abu Rabia. Translated with permission by Naji Dhaher.

crowded the shoulder. But instead of cruising by, the policeman pulled alongside him and shot him an angry look. The respected journalist shook his head as if to say: "I have cleared the way for you." This incensed the officer, who shouted for him to stop. He stopped. Three policemen got out of the car, one behind the other. Together they formed a small army. An officer approached him. The reporter smiled and said: "Why did you stop me? I thought you wanted to pass."

Annoyed and nervous, the reporter reflexively patted his pocket. The feel of his papers gave him some relief. Nothing was missing.

The officer glared at him with undisguised hatred. It was certain that this was a Jewish officer. It was certain that he would accuse him of something. He would not let him go without paying a price.

The officer turned to him and spoke: "No, I did not want to pass you. I stopped you because you committed an offense."

He ordered him to show his identification and the car's papers. The officer looked at the papers and took them to his car. What did the officer want, and what evil wind sent this officer to me at the end of a busy day? He murmured to himself, praying that this was only a routine check. He tried to convince himself that the officer would see that his papers were fine and let him go home after a hectic day at the journal.

The reporter smiled to conceal his fear. The officer returned, repeating sharply: "You committed an offense."

He looked at the officer with question marks in his eyes. He wanted to ask him: "Did I commit a violation? What violation? I have been driving for thirty years. I am not a child. Check my record. It is clean."

The policeman continued: "You did not give the right of way at the junction."

How could he reply? He would tell him that he gave the right of way. For evidence, he would say no one hit their brakes, no one honked. Or he could ask instead: Who told you I did not give the right away? You were not there, yet here you are stopping me a full kilometer from the junction. What should he do? Should he contradict a police officer? Or should he be silent to ease the blow?

After a period of tension, the reporter spoke plainly: "I did not commit a violation."

The officer glared at him, ground his teeth, and said: "Yes. You committed a violation."

Behind these words, the reporter heard what wasn't said: All Arabs are liars. He looked at the officer carefully, and quickly tried to hide what he was looking for. He wanted to tell the officer that I am an old man, and not a young man who commits such a violation. But he again spoke plainly: "Believe me, sir, I was driving within the law. I just finished my work at the newspaper."

The officer gritted his teeth. It was clear that he had already decided to write the ticket. No language in the world would protect the reporter from punishment for an offense he did not commit.

As the reporter took the violation ticket and put it aside, disturbing thoughts touched his mind. His wife had accused him yesterday of driving too fast and threatened to bring the police. Recently, the mayor of his city called on the police to address the traffic problem. The mayor should have known that he was inviting the police to punish Arabs. After all, those who live outside the law know how to deal with the police, and how to commit offense after offense out in the open without consequences. The resourceful ones, he knew many of them, know how to blend in. He knew one man who drove his car without a license for over a decade and a half, and the police arrested him only after another car collided into his. Of course, the mayor should also have known that he was asking the police to solve a problem that doesn't exist—Nazareth was already one of the safest cities to drive in.

Tired of these pointless recriminations, the reporter floored the accelerator and the Cortina's engine raced. He would soon be home. He would tell his wife that he was subjected to injustice and insult for no reason except that he was an Arab living under Israeli rule. He would tell his wife that the police officer cited him without cause, that he was like a character in a novel by the great Jewish writer Franz Kafka who was caught in an inhuman system and faced an impossible trial. Yes, he would tell his wife what the charges were, if he only knew himself.

It wasn't until he glided to a stop outside his building that he noticed another group of policemen sitting in their cars, next to the building. Another storm of questions burst into his head. New fear crowded out his anger and confusion. Was today a police day? Were these people here to add more to his suffering?

He considered turning his car around and driving away, but a strange desire, buried deep in his soul, drove him to experience this torment to its fullest. It pushed him to park his car in his designated spot, in front of the building. He walked slowly past the police cars. He was tense, ready for anything. But nothing happened.

As the reporter climbed the stairs of his house, his earlier frustration returned. His wife met him at the door and immediately asked him what was wrong. He said he'd tell her later. She insisted, so he told her about how he was harassed by the passing policemen, who could have left him alone. He, a respected journalist, punished for being a barbaric Arab.

His wife put her hand on his back gently and spoke with a soothing voice: "They are backwards. They should have left you alone."

She hoped evening coffee would calm his nerves, but he was clearly still agitated when he asked about the police outside the building. Speaking calmly, she explained: "They are waiting for the husband of our neighbor, Taroub, the beautiful woman. They say they have only been married a few months, and she called the cops on him. Apparently, they had a disagreement."

He looked at his wife, joking: "I thought you finally carried out your threat to report my speeding."

His wife smiled: "If you speed again I will call the police. This time you are forgiven."

The prominent journalist and his wife shared a laugh, and then the journalist went alone to his dark room. He had tears in his eyes, but they would not fall.

PART 3

The Owl Neighborhood

A NOVELLA

NAJI DHAHER

THE OWL NEIGHBORHOOD

1

Tumult, turmoil, uproar, battlefields and battles all signify one thing: War. Yes, it is war. That is how we, the sons of the Palestinian family whose fathers were expelled from their homeland, have felt all along. As you know, the war lays down its burden. What is this eloquent expression, "lays down its burden?" Hah! No one can tell the winner from the loser. We are all winners and we are all losers! Yet we all prefer to escape this confession so that we will not revel in each other's misfortune. How can we submit to the idea of being conquered? How can my life go on if I admit my defeat, and my opponent, even if it is my wife, knows it, and so invites drummers and flute players to come to celebrate my downfall? I do not know. But one day I did it. I confessed my defeat and did not think twice before leaving my house waving the white flag so the wide world could welcome me and my undoing.

Such was the beginning, my child, and what followed is not known to you. Mine is a long story, which, I think, would take a long time to tell. If you wish, I will tell it to you. Are you shaking your head? What do you mean? Do you not want to hear my whole story? OK. I will grant your wish. The short version is this: I have returned after years of absence to be among you. It is true that all of you, especially your mother, have been hard on me, but still I want to return to you. I want to root my existence in your midst. I want to see your two sisters to verify that the younger, who is like Haifa Wehbe, has grown up to become a vision of honor and beauty. As for the older one, who has an Indian face, shape and smile, I am sure her beauty is causing you some headaches.

Trust me, my child. I miss everything. From my grave, even your mother and her battles have become pleasant memories. She is the source of the stories I tell to amuse my neighbors. I have become famous, thanks to my stories about her. I have told these stories to my neighbors' neighbors and all of them want me to tell these stories to their neighbors now. I have become famous among the dead. Whenever my name is mentioned, smiles appear, as if each smile says that this man knows how to tell a sad story that can amuse us through our pain.

Are you getting tired of my story? Do you want me to wrap it up? How difficult this is! How difficult, my child, it is for the Arab man to be an outsider in face, hand, and tongue! Alright! Don't talk to me about hardships, for I am familiar with them. I have known them very well and I am ready to cope. The road I've travelled bearing the flag of defeat from my house to my resting place and back has strengthened me. My suffering has made me valiant, not to be matched by even Antarah[1] in his prime. My child, I want to go back home. I long for the meals of your damned mother! I especially long for the plates of eryngoes, artichoke, and herbs. Your mother excelled in cooking the artichoke following the advice of her mother, who told her, "If you need a break from his complaining, cook him this meal." Indeed, I long for her, damn her! I miss her shouting and wailing which filled the house and the neighborhood. I miss her breaking vases, her throwing my gifts out our window, as she hurled her many vivid curses at me within. Damn her! She was good hearted, very sweet! I did not understand that until my exile.

Where are you going, my child? Our home is in the eastern neighborhood, why are you taking me to the west? Did you move there after I left? You deserve to live there! Indeed, why not? Your mother benefited a lot from the West. So she deserves to live in the western neighborhood. The West inspired the government to pass the women's protection law. Since the day I told your mother that this law gave a woman the right to throw her husband out of the house, our life became a living hell. Your mother stopped cooking my favorite dish and sought neither my satisfaction nor my dead mother's. Whenever we had an argument, even the mildest, she would go into my room, mess up her hair exactly like an ogre's and rush straight to the police station. The police at times believed her story and at other times did not,

1 A pre-Islamic poet and knight.

but, once they realized that she came to the station repeatedly without any signs of violence on her body, they started to ignore her claims. Afterwards, your mother discovered the way to the court where I said before the judge that I would stay away from home. Upon hearing my statement, she smiled, put a piece of gum in her mouth and said, "I don't want to live with this man." So, I raised the white flag and had no choice but to go away, far away.

Is our home here? In the western neighborhood? Go in! We are now on the third floor? Your mother is Westernized, my child. I swear by *Allah* she is Westernized. I mean she has become a Westerner. She has moved away from our Arab life. She sold the house whose price was the blood of my heart. Did she sell it to buy this place on the third floor? Where did you go my child? Why did you leave me in this maze and go away? Do you think I can climb these red, confusing stairs? I know you can do it. Your sister, Haifa Wehbe, and the Indian-faced one can do it, too. But do you think I can do it? OK, I will try; I can lose nothing. Oh, *Allah*, help me! My child! The stairs are trembling under my feet. Is it possible I am so old? Or is it my legs which are shaking, not the stairs? Can I climb your mother's stairs? On Him we rely, no worries. Ouch! My foot has slipped. Help me! Aren't you my child? By *Allah*, whenever I saw you, as a child, fall on the ground, my heart would drop down between my feet and not return to its place until I was sure you were OK, and now you, my child, don't have the patience to stay with me until I reach the third floor, your mother's floor! Never mind. I am holding the handrail. I have saved myself. Speaking of saving, you don't know your father's will and strength. You see? I have regained my balance and here I am placing my foot on the step once again. I am going up, up, but where am I going? Do these stairs have no end? Has your mother found out that my ghost has come back? Has she found refuge in the West and its laws, which can return my ghost to its place? No! No! My child. I have a feeling that your mother has changed. Only the stone doesn't change. Your mother is not a stone; she is a mass of emotions. I know her well. Who knows her better than I? She, like us, lives in a forced exile. The West deceived her with its laws. But I am confident that the smell of the land of our village, Sirin, will return her to her roots, to her eryngoes, artichokes, and herbs. I am confident, my child.

That's why I insist on returning to her and to home. I am also confident that life is more powerful than death. You know that I have been familiar with both and that I am clinging stubbornly to life because it is the stronger. Ouch! My leg has slipped once again off the red step. Will you hold my hand? Where have you gone? Ouch! Here again I have regained my balance. I am the finest of the youth! See? Should I keep going upward till I reach your mother, the mistress of beauty and elegance? Listen! Isn't it a fact that whoever loves beauty should give away his soul and money? This is what Abdel Wahab [2] said. But do you think that Abdel Wahab is more courageous than your father? No, my child. Your father is a strong man. His dreams have always been great. When your father decides to reach a goal, he reaches it no matter how long the road is. Besides, don't ever forget that your father traveled the hardest of roads: the road of storytelling! He managed to make the dead nod their heads in admiration. Your father is not just a mere father! He has endurance and can accomplish what he sets out to accomplish.

Should I climb another step? Another step and that's it? Indeed, I have arrived; I have arrived at the kitchen window. The window is open. I can get through. I want to do it. That's why I am here. Who is that? Is that your mother? Is it possible that she has been working in the kitchen since I left her a few years ago? Damn her! She hasn't changed a bit. She is still tying the kerchief on her forehead. It looks like a man's headband. Look! She is still holding a knife and cutting things. Damn you, woman! You must have cut a great many things in your life! No one in this world has suffered from your practice of cutting more than me. Your mother, my son, has not yet seen me. She is busy cutting things. Ouch, ouch! My leg has slipped once more. Now I am hanging in the air. If I fall off the third floor in the western neighborhood, I will return to my grave. Your mother hears me. I feel there are words in her eyes. She does not want to see me. Neither estrangement, nor distance, nor even death enabled her to forgive me. What did I do to you, woman of noble origin? We, the Arabs, receive our enemies and the slayer of our children when they enter

---

2 A popular twentieth-century Egyptian musician.

our houses. Aren't you an Arab? Don't you want to see me? Alright, lady of beauty and elegance, that's your right, as the Jewish woman judge said. I know that no one can force somebody else to live with him. I know all. But I thought that separation might change you. I know. I know. It is difficult for a person to change. But see! I have changed. Do you think I went away before the tumult because I was fond of leaving? Or that I left because there was another woman in my life? No, my son! It wasn't at all like that. You know I am the son of a family forced into exile. I did my best to give Haifa Wehbe the chance to dance at our home and her sister the opportunity to sing you the songs you loved from Indian films, full of sadness and love. I am exhausted and have suffered many trials. Perhaps I made a mistake when I believed you were strong like me. Perhaps I was wrong. But I have already paid the price for the Jews and the West where the Jews came from. What more can I do? I am here for a visit, a short visit after which I will return to my infinite space, the space of the dead and their stories. Damn you, woman! You don't want me to enter the house!? Do you still believe there is another woman in my life? No! There is no woman or anything else in my life. What you thought was a woman was my dream for you and your children to live a comfortable life. I was doing nothing but devilling in the wilderness of stories, hoping to write one that could lift us upward. The other woman was none but the writer in me, the writer with a head full of stories. I was running after another story, not after another woman, and perhaps the only woman in that story was you, fool! You don't believe me? Are you waving the knife in my face? Won't you receive me after all these years? Will you send me tumbling from your kitchen window to my other world? Has your hatred reached this point? Alright. Alright. The West taught you it is your right to hate the man who is your husband and the father of your children. They told you that is your right. Ouch! Ouch! I am dangling from the third floor. I am about to fall. You won't take my hand? Is this really it? I am going to fall. I won't see my daughter, Haifa Wehbe's twin, or the Indian-dark-faced one; in fact, I won't see anybody again, not even my young child who has guided me to this new house in the western neighborhood with its red stairs. I won't see anyone anymore. Where have you gone my child?

Husam waited way too long for his father, Raqraq al-Sharif, to come back out. The young son was circling around the building, like a bird flying around its nest. He gazed at the darkness inquisitively, longing for answers to his questions: Where are you now, my father? What happened to you? I should not have left you alone with such a cruel and heartless woman, who married another man as if nothing had happened right after you, my father, left. I should not have left you. I grew up, father! I grew up and became a young man. I have experienced the turmoil of life. I am no longer that naive boy. The days of my mother speaking ill of you and slandering you in front of upper-class society and ordinary folks are gone. I am a capable young man, and I will not allow the past to be repeated. The time of insults is gone. You'll see, it's the beginning of a new era. You'll see, dad, I will show you how I trample the heads of anyone who insults or belittles you. You raised our heads high, my twin sisters, Shafiqha and Rafiqah, and I. We are proud to be your children, whenever your name is mentioned you are recognized as the great writer. We are all so proud of you and now the time has come for us to repay you for the rewards of your good name and great kindness.

As Husam formed these thoughts, a strange aura descended on the place. An owl landed in a treetop nearby enshrouded in the sudden fog. Its call pierced the darkness, portending some evil event. Husam looked in every direction, but he could not see through the enveloping gloom. He walked toward the owl's cry and was astonished to see a cat with its fur on end walking slowly as if to guide him to the mysterious visitant. As Husam followed the cat to the entrance of the building, he sensed something unfamiliar and strange. His dread increased as the cat meowed loudly before the door. What has happened to your father and what is awaiting you, son of the calamity? Feelings of uneasiness overtook the young man as he followed the strange cat through the mist.

Naji Dhaher, *The Owl Neighborhood,* trans. Hazza Abu Rabia. Translated with permission by Dar Al-Mal Publishing House.

There, before the wall of the building, where his mother Zeina al-Sha'sha'a lived, he heard a man moaning. His heart told him that it was his father's voice. He examined his surroundings carefully, but saw nothing. The cat disappeared momentarily before stealing up behind him. Are these, in fact, the cries of my father? If they are, where is he?

"Look! I am here, my child."

His father's voice split the darkness. Husam followed the moaning from the ground up where he saw his father hanging by the tip of his collar on an iron rod. Perhaps the contractor left it there, to build an addition that never got built. Husam extended his hand, barely reaching his father's shoe.

"Be careful, my child. This iron bar frightens me. I cannot see the ground, it may be full of other bars," said the voice.

The son looked around frightened. His heart raced as he found a ladder leaning against the nearby wall. He carried the ladder towards his father's voice with infinite affection. "Come on good ladder, come on. Thank goodness for the hands that placed you here, as if they had anticipated such a predicament."

Husam brought the ladder close to his father's dangling body. He ascended the steps cautiously, guided by the overwhelming thought that his father was responsible for his existence in this finite world. As he climbed, he brought his father's face closer to his own, and he saw the shadow of a smile looming on his lips. "Behold father, I have reached you, soon you will be safe. The moment of danger is behind us. I will not let you fall whatever the cost." His father's smile grew clearer. The son approached the iron rod and freed his father from it. His father's body slumped on the son's shoulder. The only thing left for him was to descend the ladder step by step.

When he arrived at the bottom step, he marveled at his achievement. He had saved his father's very existence. He lowered the relaxed body from his shoulder to the ground. When he grasped his father's hand to reassure him that the moment of danger had passed, he was startled by a feeling of warmth and wetness. He pulled his hand back and saw his father's blood. With all his strength, Husam ripped his right shirtsleeve and gently wrapped his father's right hand. Then he ripped off his other sleeve for his father's other hand.

The wounded father noticed that his son was nearly hysterical with concern. He held his son's hand in his wounded hands and said:

"Do not be afraid, my child. Your mother only wanted to get rid of me. That's why these cuts are not too deep. Do not be afraid; my wounds are trivial and will soon heal."

The son looked at his father's face, which was beaming in the deep darkness. The father smiled and said: "I thought you had left me to face my destiny alone."

A tear fell from the son's eye as he replied: "Father, did you ever leave me to face my destiny alone? Have you forgotten how you raised me, shielding me with your tears? No father, I will never forget. I am your little one who grew up, I have never forgotten. I did not follow you to mother's house because I did not want to see her insult you as she has in the past. That's why I left you to ascend those steps alone. I did not abandon you. I watched patiently in the darkness for your return."

The grieving father said: "Do not say this, my child. Your mother was not so cruel to you, not to this extent."

Husam replied in a strained voice, as if he wanted to hide a secret: "Dad, who said that she was not cruel. Who said this?"

His father did not answer, but instead asked: "What did you do in my absence? Say it son and put me at ease."

Reluctant to share such disturbing news, the son, at last, responded: "Dad, my mother married someone who does not come close to your character. Her new husband is a criminal and drug addict. That son of a bastard divided our family and got rid of us one by one and became the patriarch and now he does whatever he wants."

"Is it true my child?" the father asked.

"It is the truth, father. My mother married Sama'an al-Atrash. Please, father, I don't want you to be angry. It's time to stop the cycle of anger you've suffered throughout your cruel life."

"The good man, my child, only blames as much as he loves. He doesn't get flustered, because he knows that anger is a force that separates one from the other."

After a short silence, he continued: "Did she really marry Sama'an al-Atrash?" Husam looked at his father with great sympathy, but before the loving son could comfort his father, a bucket of cold water drenched them both. The screaming voice from the third floor announced the start of another battle.

3

"What happened? Does the rain fall in our summer?" Raqraq al-Sharif inquired of his son.

The son, Husam, smiled and extended his hands into the dark space in front of him and said: "You did not hear her voice roaring from above?"

The father went into his shell, and started to think about his wife, how she has not changed and will not change. The days go on in the world of transformation and alteration and she remains exactly as she was. She only cares about living the way she wants. The time of the Palestinians is over; this is the era of the Israelis who came from overseas. The Israelis came up with strange and bizarre laws and imposed them upon the indigenous people of the country, disavowing our customs and the old relationships between man and woman.

"Why did they do that? Is it because of their love of freedom or because they want to destroy our society which is totally different from the societies that embraced them and educated them?

"Freedom or destruction. Maybe both. And maybe these two motives combined led Zeina to reject me, her loyal husband," al-Sharif said to himself. He repeated himself, as if the idea would otherwise escape, "Maybe the two things together." He continued: "Who knows, our ways may not be in their consideration. Maybe the courts are just another battlefield in the great war, the mother of all wars between them and us." Al-Sharif learned long ago that the time of Palestinian men was over. You must be with your wife, beside her. If not, the best thing you can do is to find some other place where you can preserve your dignity. He had warned his friends about the new law regarding women's rights. He never thought that he would be the law's first victim. The day had arrived when she would roundly berate him, then threaten to go to the police and to court, and indeed that is what happened.

He did not know how to respond to this new world. What could he do about a world where your wife could throw you from a building and dump cold water on your head? He did not know how to proceed. All his thoughts were dead ends. Where was his home and his old life? Simply gone? Should he collect his tales and flee from this hostile place? The question was difficult, so he preferred not to answer right away. Who knows? Maybe the answer will come after an exhausting day or from the mouth of a homeless wandering cat who does not have any protection. My time is not up yet. If, in the end, I must go back to my graveyard, it won't be today. Now I must prepare for another confrontation with this westernized woman. She gave up on me, but I have not given up on her.

Husam asked his father: "What do you think, Dad?"

The father answered: "What do I think, my child? I think as you think."

Father and son exchanged a meaningful smile and did not say another word. Husam was a grown man who realized that you cannot run from your problems. Buoyed by pride in his son, Raqraq turned again to face his predicament. Where will I go? How will I prepare myself for the conflict in my home and in my land?

As soon as the father opened his mouth to speak, the owl extended its wings and glided into the darkness. The two laughed and asked themselves if the owl, too, had been forced to flee by a sudden cold rain. With no better ideas, the men followed the owl instinctively. In whatever ruined land she alights, they too would stay, waiting for unknown events to unfold.

They ran through the night, following the owl, and finally stopped in the middle of the nearby forest. Here they caught their breath and contemplated their next move in an unequal confrontation between themselves, two unarmed men, and a Socratic woman backed by an armed government with soldiers and weapons, ready to break the biggest ego in the neighborhood.

The two were very tired and slumped against the tree where the owl landed. They closed their eyes, both of them thinking of how to face that ungracious woman, the wife and mother who lives at the top of the red stairs. In his own way, each imagined that he had somehow managed to reverse time and return home to the old sweet life, even if the old home could never be quite as warm as it once was.

During this reverie, the father's thoughts rested on his twin dazzling daughters, Shafiqa and Rafiqa, who speak with one voice, and he peered into the darkness as if he expected to find them there.

"What has happened to them?"

Husam turned his head in the dark and asked: "Dad, what are you ranting about? Who?"

The father continued to stare into the darkness: "No, my child, your father does not rant, it is too early for ranting. There is still time to think. There are people who I love, and I need to ask about them. Not because I want to solve my problems through them. But because they are dear to my heart, I must ask about them. They matter to me even if the whole world denies them, including your mother."

The son returned to his own thoughts. A father remains a father, regardless of how the days have treated him. "Dad, you want to be reassured about your little girls? I will tell you what happened to them. They were married to twin brothers who are like them in so many ways. Yes, father, their spouses are similar to them. As soon as you meet them, you will see. They have done well by escaping the house of Sama'an al-Atrash. Mother long ago surrendered to his rudeness and madness. She could not protect her daughters from his unpredictable violence."

The son's silence was long and the darkness in the forest became heavier. Raqraq's confusion showed in his sensitive eyes. Though he had no reassuring thoughts to share, Husam felt compelled to lift his father's burden or, at least, stir him from his painful reflections. Looking not at his father but into the surrounding darkness, the son spoke with a father's firm voice: "Later, let us talk about my sisters, later, Dad. Right now, we must focus on what awaits us."

After a short pause, he continued: "Do you insist on going back home, Father?"

The father had a resentful look on his face. "Is there any other possibility? Of course, I will return to our home. Where would I go if not there? I believe, my child, that your mother will one day wake up from her drunkenness, open the door, and welcome me, her husband, the father of her sons. And we will discover together, she and I, that what happened was a long nightmare and is now the past."

Darkness surrounded them on all sides, and confusion was evident in the son's face. He was absorbed in his grief. "Dad, I wish that it were all a nightmare and would go away. It seems that you did not learn from the past, however. The realities of Zeina al-Sha'sha'a and Sama'an al-Atrash, are not so easily undone. The feeling of peace during battle is nothing more than foolishness. Dad, be attentive to what the moments bring to you. Be vigilant and brave, the confrontation is coming and it is inevitable."

A forest breeze carried these feelings from father to son, and steeled the father for the next confrontation. Are stories truly stories without conflict?

At that moment, they lay back to back, facing outward toward the forest, to protect themselves from the unknown. That night, they slept with eyes wide open.

Before morning, the bleary father asked: "And what are we supposed to do?"

The son responded immediately without turning to his father: "It's time to face the problem together."

At the top of the tree, the owl screeched into the night, a portent of approaching evil.

4

As the two were sleeping fitfully, the owl flew to a nearby neighborhood and landed near the living room window of the home of Zeina al-Sha'sha'a, the unruly wife and distant mother. Zeina entered the room, slamming the door behind her and tossing her handbag toward the living room sofa. It landed with a thud, arousing her new husband, Sama'an al-Atrash, from a light sleep. He strode into the room angrily, stood in front of his wife, and asked: "Can't you stop being so noisy? You're disturbing me. Can no one rest tonight?"

Caught off guard, Zeina struggled to respond. This brief delay incensed Sama'an, who yelled viciously: "I am telling you, I am not telling the wall!"

Defiant herself, Zeina ignored this demand and went about her business. A wave of rage engulfed her husband. He grabbed her hair with both hands: "I am not one of those who is disobeyed by a woman, come here!" He beat her severely, hitting her all over her body with his heavy hands. When his arms tired, he began to bite her, stopping at her bottom. Now this lesson will have maximum effect, he thought, and he bit her there hard.

Zeina screamed desperately and begged him to stop. He continued until she promised him never to act that way again. He finally left her alone and said: "That's how I like you."

After a period of silence, he added: "I think you know my character well by now. I'm not like your foolish husband. Just try to go to the police, if you do your end will be on my hands."

Recovering her senses, Zeina grabbed the coffee kettle from the kitchen counter. She held it in her hand and asked her husband to be patient. "I will prepare a cup of coffee to calm your temper," she said softly.

Moments later, they sat side-by-side. Zeina poured coffee into a cup and handed it to her husband. She then poured coffee into another cup and brought it close to her mouth, but she did not drink it.

"Do you know what happened today?"

"How should I know? I was not there."

"Raqraq al-Sharif, my ex-husband, tried to break into the apartment while I was here."

"What did you say? Your husband tried to break into the apartment? Raqraq al-Sharif was here? Didn't you tell me he was dead?"

"Yes, he died. We buried him and put a mountain of dirt and stones on top of his body. I don't know what happened. He is like a cat with nine lives. He loses one, but he lives on."

"How did he try to break in?"

"He tried to come through the kitchen window, but I stopped him by cutting his fingers. He fell towards the ground, but not all the way. He caught the bar of iron on the side of the building and hung on until Husam brought him down. Husam wrapped his father's wounded hands with his shirt sleeves. To teach him a lesson about coming around here, I doused him with icy water."

Her husband asked her eagerly: "Have they tried to come back again?"

"No, they haven't tried. Even if they did, they couldn't because I am on the lookout for them. You don't trust that I can teach them a lesson and make them forget what once was?"

The husband finished his coffee, and when his wife tried to refill his cup he motioned for her to stop. He stood up and abruptly left the room, leaving his wife confused. Will this story end with peace or more violence, she wondered?

In vain, Sama'an al-Atrash tried to sleep, but he was kept awake by the strange story of his wife's husband resurrected from the cities of death. Where did this dangerous man come from? Why he did come? Sleep was impossible, so he got up before dawn. He could not leave things unresolved even if it meant wrestling with a ghost. Get rid of your enemy before he gets rid of you!

He opened his wardrobe, dressed himself, retrieved his helmet from its hiding place in the closet and put it on. He grabbed the pipe near the window, and a few moments later he was sprinting to his motorcycle parked behind the building. Before he could reconsider, he was speeding toward the forest.

Sama'an al-Atrash knew how to get rid of his adversaries. He knew of more than one way to put an end to anyone who defies him. His method on this night was to drive back and forth on the road between the forest and his house. At around 3:00 am, Sama'an saw a man with shabby clothes emerge from the forest and continue down the adjoining street. As the man approached the middle of the road, it was clear to Sama'an that it was his enemy Raqraq al-Sharif. He recognized the man's wounded hands, which were wrapped in shirtsleeves. He accelerated towards him at crazy speed, braking just in time to hurt but not kill his stunned enemy, who landed hard at the edge of the forest. Sama'an stood over Raqraq and spoke sharply: "This is your first warning. If you don't stay away from this neighborhood, expect worse."

***

Raqraq al-Sharif lay still on the edge of the forest, under the trees. The blow was so powerful that if he had not been alerted at the last moment, he would have been back in the cemetery, among his beloved. God protected him. This was not the end. His pain assured him that the wretched still have time in their lives. The crucial moment between life and death will not be delayed or come a moment too early. Thank God I wasn't seriously hurt, he thought. Raqraq al-Sharif tried to stand on his two legs but couldn't. Walking was out of the question. He tried to crawl, but he found it impossible to move without pain.

He closed his eyes and thought about what had happened to him just now and the day before. Wouldn't it have been safer to remain among his fellow dead? As he lay with his thoughts, a droplet of water fell from the top of the tree above him giving his body a sense of life. He looked up and saw the owl from his neighborhood peering down, as if to reassure him. He knew that it was the owl that had dropped the water of life to restore his sense of delightful existence. He lowered his gaze, then quickly looked up towards the tree another time, trying to surprise the owl and catch her reaction, but she did not move. He then felt safe. There is someone in the world that understands him. It is true that his wife denied him despite his kindness to her, but the Lord beats with one hand and protects with the other. God protected us, my good owl, and without his protection I wouldn't be here.

The owl swooped down and brought her beak close to al-Sharif's mouth. His lips opened without his even realizing it, and water spread warmth throughout his body. What a wonderful feeling when someone cares about your existence in the world and comforts you with a sip of water! He looked at the owl's eyes and saw infinite tenderness. He now realized that he had a companion to relieve him from the hardships of his former life. He extended his hand, and the owl came closer. Gratitude overwhelmed him. The forest glowed and the nearby flowers bloomed, as if to celebrate this fabulous bond.

Raqraq al-Sharif was overwhelmed. Joy flooded the forest as far as he could see. The wounded man saw a shadow moving towards him. It was his son, Husam, who came right on time. The beaten man stood suddenly on his two legs and ran to his son. He forgot that moments before he had been unable to walk or even crawl. A miracle had occurred, and he was rejuvenated.

Husam approached his father, while the owl flew to the top of the tree to take her place for the decisive battle between those whom she loved and those whom it seemed she didn't.

"What happened, my father? A little while ago I heard a rumble that could shake a mountain, what happened?" Husam asked.

His father replied: "An unexpected setback. Just as I started down the road, a man on a motorcycle ambushed me. He rushed toward me like a storm and knocked me right back to the forest." Raqraq looked up at the owl and continued, "I do not know why I feel that this owl saved my life. But I owe her my existence here and now. I think that the motorcyclist is your mother's husband, Sama'an al-Atrash, or a person related to him. As I flew through the air, I felt hatred surrounding me. I remember him saying something like, 'This is a warning.'"

Husam embraced his father, thanking God for his safety: "Sounds like my mother's husband. It was definitely Sama'an al-Atrash. The people call him this because he does not listen to anyone. He responds to words with violence. Those who know him know his aggression well."

The father smiled. When the son asked him why he was smiling, he replied: "For many years I thought your mother was attracted to this type of violent man. She does not prefer the polite writer type. That's the root of our problems. I am quite certain of it. It seems that I am better suited to the company of the owl, and my talks with her will have to console me."

The father and son were surrounded by an aura of calm and affection. "Praise be to *Allah* for your safety, Father. Praise be to *Allah*! From this moment on, we must be more careful."

"How can we be more careful, my child? What good would it do in a world where evil has descended on the people? We suffer from our enemies' laws and underhanded tactics, like those that the motorcyclist used on me a moment ago."

The son looked at his father with love and concern. These two days reminded him how much he appreciated him. His father is a respected writer, only choice words flow from his mouth, like those he whispered in his ear before. Saying perhaps more than he should, the son spoke plainly: "We must expect more evil from those who fill the earth with anger and hatred. We must keep our eyes open so we can avoid them before they hurt us."

As the son spoke, the owl glided down from the top of the tree as if to say that she agreed with the wise young man, who was trying to protect both his father and a history, which has every right to survive under the warm sun.

5 ——————————————————————————————

A while ago, there were two people in the forest: the father, Raqraq al-Sharif, and his son, Husam. Now there are three if you count the owl, their new friend. It's true that the owl was present with them, though only gradually did they accept that the owl protected them from atop her tree. Physical presence is not the same as spiritual presence, and from al-Sharif's point of view, spiritual presence is the more important of the two. Wasn't Raqraq al-Sharif physically present with his wife, Zeina al-Sha'sha'a? Didn't they live together for years and years under one roof? Didn't they bear sons and daughters? Yes, all of this happened. However, the days revealed to him that he was a foolish husband. They were not joined in spirit. It was evident the minute he left his wife, Zeina al-Sha'sha'a. She quickly re-married a thick-headed yob who only listens to what he wants to hear, Sama'an al-Atrash, may God make him deaf.

Father and son were overcome with joy as they realized they were no longer alone. They hugged each other with true affection, embracing as they never had before. The great fear that followed them through the forest had lifted. They rested on the forest floor free from concerns and troubles.

The father looked up to the top of the tree where he saw his owl standing like a guard outside the doors of the virtuous city. He thanked God for this blessing. He thanked God that he was again, at last, close to the house, which was once his home.

He said to his son without looking at him: "Now we can sleep well."

"No father, we cannot sleep. Since I saw you again a short while ago, I've been waiting to tell you something important."

"Son, it's been a while since we could sleep well and now we can."

"That's true father, many times we slept with our eyes wide open. However, there is something that I have to talk to you about."

The father retreated within himself. What does he want to say in this deep darkness? Is it a new story that completes an old one? Why can't it wait until morning? Have mercy on us, Lord. Have mercy on us, on my son and me, please deliver us from the error that we brought to ourselves.

The son noticed that his father was tense and tried to ease his mind: "Do not worry, father. If what I am about to say bothers you, I can postpone it. Even if the delay wastes an opportunity that does not come along every day."

The father was perplexed: "What does this Husam say? Why does he speak so mysteriously? Why this enigma? Certainly, there is something that shouldn't be delayed, and possibly the opportunity might not come again in my limited return to this earth." He finally asked his son: "Why do you make me so curious to listen and yet hesitate to say what you want to say?"

"Oh Father, do you promise to remain calm, as you always have?"
The father replied: "What? You ask me to promise to remain calm! You don't know me yet, my son? You don't realize that I'm a writer and I know how to take in such surprises and evaluate them like someone who weighs gold." He paused for a moment and looked at his son before continuing with greater force, gaining momentum: "Husam, do you know what it means to be a writer? A writer has very keen senses, he anticipates occurrences before they happen, and he plans for the unexpected in more than one way."

Once again, the writer paused and gazed at his son. This time he asked directly: "Why do you make me more curious? Tell me! Say what you want to say, my child! I am drowning in the springs of anxiety and its tormented seas."

Husam sulked as he always did in such complicated situations and said: "It's about my twin sisters, Shafiqa and Rafiqa."

The father exclaimed from the depths of his concern: "What is it? What happened to your sisters, my child? Has anything bad happened to them? Oh, how miserable I would be if they were in danger!"

"Do not worry, dad. Do not worry so much. It's just that … ." Husam had hoped to calm his father, but he could not find the words and his effort backfired.

Raqraq al-Sharif struggled to keep his concern from spilling into anger. He spoke slowly in a measured tone: "Talk, my son. Speak, I promise to remain calm and not to do anything foolish today that I may regret tomorrow."

At last, the words began to flow from Husam's mouth. Some were understood but others eluded the father. The words flowed from the son's mouth like a waterfall cascading in all directions. Overwhelmed at first, the father had no choice but to make sense of this stunning news. Through his pain, he managed to suss out Husam's sad narrative: Shafiqa and Rafiqa, his two precious twins, returned to their mother's house, leaving their homes. Their mother, Zeina al-Sha'sha'a, offered to stay by their sides in her house. Divorce, she said, is not the end, but a beginning. It was Zeina al-Sha'sha'a's vision for this new future that so saddened her first husband. She would arrange lessons for them in dancing and singing. She would prepare a party for them attended by worthless people, yobs and perverts.

The last sentence from Husam struck his father's heart like a thunderbolt. He gazed at the owl and vowed to undo his wife's plans no matter the cost.

6

Raqraq al-Sharif carried his battered body on two anxious legs. With surprising speed, he ran through the trees, penetrating the heart of darkness, while his owl flew above him, protecting him through the cruel night.

When Raqraq decided not to leave the battlefield to Hamedan but to brave this abandoned, inhospitable place, he entered the darkness alone. He would not expose his son to harm.

The tired and worried father stopped at the red staircase of his wife's building. He climbed the red stairs ignoring the danger. This time was different. Propelled by love for his son, Raqraq put his foot on the first red stair and found himself bounding like a young man to the second and third. Finally, he reached the kitchen window. Once again, he scrambled up to the ledge where he could look inside the house without being seen. The owl perched on a wire close by and kept watch. The scene inside the house was familiar. His wife was tying her hair in a knot that nearly touched the ceiling. She sat on a low chair. His daughters wore what appeared to be eastern dancing dresses, so revealing that their bodies were exposed.

"O Lord protect my little ones, they have become two mature women. I wish they had grown up with me, close to me," he thought sadly as he wiped the trace of a tear. His owl kept watch, and Raqraq thought, "Oh, what if my wife were just like this loyal friend? What happened between us would have never happened at all, and I would be the patriarch now with his wife, daughters, and sons."

The show started. Zeina beat an Egyptian rhythm on an empty aluminum bucket, once used for storing pickles. His twin daughters responded by moving provocatively, like the dancers in bars and cabarets from Egyptian films and TV shows. The scene was full of profligacy, yet Zeina, his wife, paused her drumming only to shout encouragement: "Dance more spontaneously, I do not want a shy person's dance! Release yourselves from inhibition. I want the audience to marvel at your movements. The real dance will feed you with a gold spoon."

The twin daughters stopped dancing and spoke in harmony as they used to when they were children sitting on their mother's lap: "But how do you want us to dance, mother?"

Then their mother rose from her low chair and shimmied suggestively, swaying her whole body and moving her buttocks and chest. She danced like this until her body, face, and her hair were covered in sweat. She then stopped and yelled: "I want you to dance like I danced. I want you to be free from any constraint. Do not be languid like your cowardly father, lover of books and paper. I want you to be brave like Nadia el-Goundy.[3] Try again, but this time, really dance."

She began beating the aluminum bucket with both hands, and her daughters followed her lead. After a while, she got tired and stopped: "This bucket broke my hands. Tomorrow I will go the market to buy a durbaka, and we'll throw a party for the rich and the big traders in the country."

At this, the twin sisters laughed loudly, and the mother yelled at them: "What do you find so humorous? What is silly in what I said?"

The twin sisters replied simultaneously: "Are you sure that the people you have in mind are actually honest rich men and important businessmen?"

The mother said: "If they are not of that class, who would be then? You think they are yobs and drug traffickers?"

***

All the while, Raqraq peered from the window in disbelief. It was obvious that his wife had lost all ties to morality and become obsessed with money. What kind of woman is this and what happened to her moral compass? Was she willing to sell the honor of her daughters, her two precious twins? Even in my darkest nightmares, I never imagined that this woman could stoop so low. I must do something to help my two young ones, he thought. He looked at his wife in disgust and said: "Oh, daughter of a bastard, if you want to destroy yourself, do it, but how could you destroy our daughters? The ghoul consumed the whole

---

3 Nadia el-Goundy is an Egyptian actress who often danced and sang in her movie appearances.

world except her daughters. Which evil spirit, still worse, has entered you?" He grinded his teeth and said, "I cannot accept this! Is there no other way?"

A breeze grazed the grieving father's face, spreading sweat across his forehead. He grabbed the handkerchief from his pocket and wiped the burning sweat. His imagination took him to worlds far from here, but he was nowhere but here now. The brutal scene engrossed him: gazelles fleeing the hunters' knives. He focused his attention on the two gazelles. He ran beside them. This image distracted him, but only momentarily. He remained stuck in this terrible metaphor for minutes that felt like centuries, until the voices of his two daughters pulled him back to the present: "Mother, we want to be honest, it was us who crossed the line in our homes, not our husbands. We made a mistake mother, and we want to remedy our situations with our spouses by returning to them and our homes."

"What are you saying? May God curse the moment I met your father. It was a dark moment. Are you serious? You made a mistake and now you want to fix the mistake? Are there no men in the city? Both of you are pretty women. All the men crave your attention, and are willing to leave their lives and follow you, but apparently you are like your unnamed father who favors poverty."

She paused for a moment and then continued: "Both of you need to seriously think before we buy a durbaka. I will not accept this from you. As for that second dog, Sama'an al-Atrash, if he remains this way, I will kick him out as well and I will find another man who can offer me a better life. I am sick of the cycle of poverty."

As Zeina al-Sha'sha'a uttered her incautious words, her husband Sama'an al-Atrash entered the room and struck her: "What did you say, daughter of the bastard? Do you want to kick me out of the house as you drove that dog away? Fie upon you! I am the resilient one who will kick your daughters and that hack writer out. Since the day we married, you and your daughters have been ungrateful pigs. If you think that I am like your ex-husband, father of pen and paper, you are mistaken. I drank my mother's milk, and I will reduce you to a mangy bitch whose owner ties her outside the house."

The father, Raqraq al-Sharif, looked at his two daughters, so vulnerable in their skimpy dancing outfits. He hoped they would leave before the beating began. He couldn't bear such a sight. He might suffer a heart attack if Sama'an so much as touched them.

Suddenly, everything stopped. His daughters disappeared from view and moments later emerged wearing their normal clothes, leaving behind the apartment, which by now resembled a destroyed battlefield. The crying father clenched his jaw, breaking a tooth. He descended the red stairs and darted after his young girls like a flying bird. Could he catch up to them? He ran and ran, while the owl's eerie scream filled the neighborhood.

7

Raqraq al-Sharif rested at the edge of the forest and his friend, the owl, perched nearby. He was safe, but tired, and his jaw was throbbing. As Raqraq watched his family's destruction from the kitchen window, an uncontainable pressure had built up inside him. This pressure found release as pressure will. The aging father had no recollection of grinding his poor teeth with such impotent force. He asked himself: "Where does all this pain come from? Do our teeth have a capacity for such pain? A moment ago, they were fine. Now, they feel as if they are shattered in all directions. O Lord, have mercy on me, a poor man who has a toothache and cannot find a cure. He is separated from his beloved twin daughters, and his son Husam, who is in the heart of the forest. And now, he is filled with terrible pain and can't do anything about it. What now?"

Raqraq had no idea. What he needed first was relief. But where could he find relief in a forest at this hour of the night? Be patient and you will find it, he told himself. Wait a minute, did not your ancestors once say that courage is to be patient for one hour? Be patient and you will have what you need. Be patient, Raqraq. This is not the first time you have felt pain, and it surely will not be the last. You have overcome pain in the past, and you will overcome it when it returns in the future.

His companion on this perilous journey, the owl, noticed his pain. She beat her wings close to him, as if to relieve or, at least, acknowledge his suffering. It was comforting to know someone in this world feels your pain and understands your suffering.

"Ouch!" he shouted at the top of his voice. He shut his eyes tightly, as if to shut out the pain, but the pain remained. There, behind the cursed window, he did not feel pain like he felt right now. Do we feel the severity of the blow only when it gets cold? His toothache dulled, at last, but a burning pain took its place. Time passed as he opened and closed his eyes with his owl steadfast nearby. Darkness was everywhere, and, except for his rueful spitting, silence was everywhere, too.

Raqraq's night of suffering was finally interrupted by a rustling sound coming from the heart of the forest. Was it the maniac Sama'an al-Atrash coming to finish him? Or was it a homeless cat looking for unattended food? Only as the noise drew quite close did Raqraq discover that it was neither—it was his beloved son, Husam.

Husam saw his father lying on the ground. He approached him and said: "What's wrong, Dad? Are you OK?"

The father pointed to his mouth: "Calm down, my child. Do not worry, it seems my teeth are broken." He continued: "Do not be afraid. I will not die; the wretched usually live long lives."

Husam knelt beside his father: "Dad, open your mouth, open it wide, let me see." The father obeyed, and the son surveyed the damage. The pain was starting to subside. "Where do you hurt the most?" Husam asked.

His father replied: "This front tooth. Do you see it? Can you tell if it's fractured?"

The son looked carefully and said: "I do not see any broken teeth. They all look strong and healthy, Father."

His father relaxed his face and he said: "If my teeth are fine, where is all this pain coming from?"

The son reassured his father, sounding strangely like a dentist: "It seems that your front tooth suffered a very strong contusion. Some time ago I experienced such a blow. The pain came, I suffered, and then it disappeared like any other pain. But how did this happen, Father?"

Raqraq feigned—rather unconvincingly—a sudden fit of pain, and kept quiet, neither responding nor moving. "I will not tell you, my child, what happened there behind your mother's window. I will not burden you with my fury or my suffering. It would only distress you. You are still a young man, leave the pain for me, I can handle it."

The son understood that his father did not want to talk about that strange blow, so he tried a less direct route: "Where did you vanish to all this time? I am not used to your disappearing acts."

Unwilling to speak his family's shame, the father tried another ruse. Looking brightly at the owl, he said: "I was at a picnic with this respectable lady."

The son smiled and the father continued: "I will take her everywhere I go so that she can understand me and my ordeal. I want to present her to everyone, including the trees and the forests, and to tell them that she is my most loyal friend in the world." Raqraq was pleased with his clever response, but his smile faded as the pain returned.

The son took a packet of salt from his pocket, tore it across the top, asked his father to open wide, and poured it in: "You are lucky I still have the salt from when I injured my tooth. Now shut your mouth, and do not swallow the salt. Leave it in your mouth until I tell you to spit it out. In a few minutes, you'll be quite thirsty, but your pain will be gone."

The father was less than convinced. Again, he ground his teeth impotently. Did his son know of his shameful adventure outside the house with the red stairs? The father froze when his son mentioned a certain surprise encounter from earlier in the night. Perhaps Husam was drawing him out?

"I just saw my twin sisters Shafiqa and Rafiqa. If you came earlier, you would have met them. They flew like two arrows towards their homes and their twin husbands." The father feigned a lack of interest. He didn't want to talk about what he had just seen through the kitchen window. He said to himself: "Yes, I am dying to see them, but I will not reveal my feelings to anyone, not even my faithful son, Husam."

As they talked, the three once again entered the heart of the forest, one behind the other—the father, his son, and their friend the owl— each wondering what fate had in store.

8

The confused father and story-teller set off with his companions for the home of his twin daughters. The closer he came to the house, the more he saw himself as a single ray of light surrounded by darkness. He badly wanted to unite his family again, but he kept his wits. The seasoned card player does not play with open cards. Accordingly, Raqraq said to himself, "Since I have not yet lost, the opposite could occur. Who knows? I may just win."

Husam wished his father Godspeed at the gate and promised to find him later, and Raqraq walked alone into the courtyard of his daughters' house. If it weren't for a single dim light, which guided his steps, he would have thought the house was empty and saved himself the trouble of knocking. But the light gave him hope, so he knocked softly. The door was not latched, and it opened slightly as he knocked. The darkness within was broken, again, by a single dim light. "Is anybody here?"

No one answered, so he repeated a little louder: "Is there anybody here?"

Inside, his daughter Shafiqa lifted her head from her pillow and called to her twin sister, Rafiqa:

"Do you hear what I hear?"

Her sister replied: "That's Father's voice!"

The twin sisters replied as one: "Come in, Father, enter."

He felt a sense of a deep nostalgia for the days when his daughters were little babies. After all this time, he still felt their innocence and beauty in his veins.

He was always delighted when the twins sang songs they learned at school. What beautiful girls they were, especially when one of them was lisping or dawdling out a new word, and her twin sister was imitating her. He would fawn over his daughters and gush to his wife, their mother, over their pleasant words and sweet songs. How the past came back at that moment as if his broken home and present predicament had never been. In a reverie, Abu Husam forgot all that happened behind the window. If you asked him about it at that moment, he would have waved you off with his hands, as if to say: Do not ask, let us live this good moment, don't ruin it with explanation and interpretation.

Once again, the sisters' twinned voice rose: "Father, how long will you stand at the door?" There was nothing to do but enter, but the father paused at the threshold, reluctant to trade the charmed past for the fraught present. It was not easy to face his lost life. But, at last, he bid his owl adieu and walked toward the welcoming voice.

Raqraq walked across the room and took his seat on a narrow sofa. As he predicted, his twins, in identical outfits, greeted him as one in the form of two. The scene became more surreal when the twin husbands entered the room and addressed their father-in-law in a single deep voice: "Welcome, uncle, you have brightened our home."

The visitor's face was filled with joy. His daughters left momentarily and returned with a tray and a coffee pot. They poured coffee into cups that looked like small kettles. True to form, the husbands sipped in unison, as did the twin sisters. The father tried to time his sips to theirs, but failed. With a smile, he said to himself: "It is enough that I am trying to be part of the harmonious group." As he finished his first cup, the sisters pulled their twin husbands aside to ask for the opportunity to talk to their father about private matters. The twin husbands rose from their seats with pleasure and left for their rooms.

A wide smile spread over the furniture, which was sinking in darkness. The light began to rise, filling the space with romance.

At last, the Father spoke: "I always wanted to experience comforts like this in my daily life at my home."

His daughters replied: "We know this, Dad. That's why we kept the light low, and the atmosphere pleasant."

The father was taken aback and said: "Could it be that the atmosphere between you and your husbands wouldn't be so if I were not here?"

The sisters smiled and said: "We understand that our father wants to make sure that we are safe. Rest assured, Dad, we are no different from the rest of the people in this town. In life's transitions, there are pleasant moments and there are bad moments. Many people say that we are like our mother, Zeina al-Sha'sha'a, in many qualities and behaviors."

This was something of a shock to Raqraq. Trying to sound even-keeled, he agreed: "I know ... I know my dears! Obviously, both of you look like your mother to a large extent." He continued under his breath: "The resemblance was painfully clear when she was beating that container for you, and you were swaying as she wanted, if not as you both wished."

The two daughters said to their father: "Do not blame us, Father. You left home when we were little girls, that's why we do not resemble you as much."

The father sounded pained: "I did not leave you. I was forced out. If I did not leave, things would have been so bad that no one, not even the crazy, would believe my stories." In a very low voice he said: "Without the mercy of my dead brothers and the splendor of what I remember of impressive tales, I would never have survived."

Once again, he recalled the crazy scene in their mother's house, when they were dancing. He asked his daughters: "Are you still skillful in the art of dancing as you were in your youth?"

The two daughters replied: "Of course, father. But we are out of practice. We cannot offer a spectacular show unless our mother guides us."

"Why would you ever offer a spectacular show, and why is your mother guiding you?"

"Why would we not perform our dance for respected people? The show we have planned will be remembered in our neighborhood for years to come. Dad, won't you be there for us?"

He replied through clenched teeth: "No, I cannot come to see it."

"But why not?"

When he thought about the drug dealers and other miscreants who would attend the show, he got mad and said: "I will not come to see you dance for those yobs."

The two sisters recalled what their mother had said about the elite guests who would attend the party, and protested: "You are wrong, Dad, the house will be filled with people of wealth and distinction. Sama'an al-Atrash, the husband of my mother, will not attend anyway. It is true that my mother is impressed with him and his manhood, but she often misses you and your company."

This was too much for Raqraq to hear. He aggressively returned: "What if I told you that I do not want you to perform at all?"

The sisters stood together and said: "We are no longer little. We can decide for ourselves what we want."

The father was enraged by his daughters as he had long been enraged by his wife. He rose to his feet and walked to the door. He stopped there and said as if remembering something: "Tell me, is your mother still dancing in revealing and suggestive clothes?"

He asked this question without waiting for an answer. He found himself outside the house, with his sons-in-law in pursuit, inviting him back so they could know him better and hear his famous stories that, they said, are so full of wisdom. He promised to tell them some of these tales at another time, though he knew that this time may never come. He started back down the road that led to the forest, accompanied, of course, by his compassionate owl. As he walked, he repeated to himself: "These twin husbands resemble me in their calmness and their obvious belief in the importance of tranquility. Calm and peace are the pillars of every sound building."

9

Outside, in the arms of darkness by the empty road, the frightened father tried to process what had just happened. He laughed to himself recalling how his two daughters talked in one voice and how their husbands did the same. His presence in his daughters' house brought back memories of the glory days, the days that smiled on him and his family. He did not deny that he felt their kindness. Seeing his daughters in agreement with their spouses, even just externally, was better than seeing them in open conflict. As he reviewed what his eyes witnessed and ears heard in his daughters' home, he experienced a kind of pain. In the end, they were loyal to their mother. Worse still, they were waiting on her signal to perform in that dirty party. Watching them rehearse had nearly destroyed him. To summarize what he now concluded: His two daughters are headed down the path of ruin just like his own family years ago. Can the husbands possibly accept that their wives will perform at a belly dance party for elites and yobs? How will they respond when the coming storm finally reaches their home? Life under continuous dispute does not last long. When the crucial moment comes, the oppressed party must decide that it is time to raise the banner of disobedience and confront the enemy.

He sent a baffled look into the darkness that surrounded him. He felt a strange kind of anger. He felt in his heart that the danger, which destroyed his home, would one day come and destroy his twin daughters' home, as well. He forgot his previous pain and ground his teeth with fresh intensity. The pain, this time, was more severe than before.

He sped toward the heart of the forest, as if he could out-race his suffering. When he saw his son, he exclaimed: "Catch me!"

He fell on the ground. Alarmed by this sudden collapse, Husam assumed the worst and ran like a madman to gather his suffering father in his arms: "What's wrong, Father? What happened to you? Please speak!"

Raqraq was weary and in great pain, but conscious. When he asked for salt, his son's face lit up. This was not the end. Husam reached into his pocket and sprinkled the contents of another packet into his father's mouth.

"Sprinkle more!" he yelled, "I'll need a factory of salt to kill this dreaded pain." Under his breath, he said: "Thank you, but is it possible not to press so severely on my teeth?"

The son sprinkled more salt into his father's mouth as he was saying to himself: "We may actually need a factory, or possibly several factories of salt before we recover from this pain. Do you think, Father, that I don't know the reason for your pain? Believe me, I know it. I passed through this experience before, and I suffered as you do. But what can we do when we not only face a woman, but also a government that is steeped in alien laws imported from the West."

The pain eased slowly. After a time, the father relaxed, closed his eyes, and fell asleep. When he opened his eyes after what he thought was a short time, he asked his son who was lying next to him how long he had slept. The son replied: "You slept some hours."

The father's face tensed: "Really? I felt that I had slept only a few moments."

The son said: "It doesn't matter. The most important thing is that you are feeling comfortable." Then as if he remembered something he said: "Did the pain ease?" The groggy father gave his son a reassuring look. He was stretching his aching bones when he noticed a letter sticking out of his son's pocket. He pointed to it and asked, "What is this?" His son told him that the police sent the father a request for an interview at the station. The police requested an investigation?

Strange, he never assaulted anyone, but many people have assaulted him. The first time he was assaulted was when his wife cut his hands with a knife; hours later, a motorcyclist knocked him into the forest, nearly killing him. And now, his beloved twin daughters treated him like a strange man, forgetting that he is dying to see them live comfortably in their home with their twin spouses. "What a strange world!" he said to himself. But what could he do? He folded the investigation letter into his pocket and went to the police station. On the way, he opened the envelope to find out what he was up against, and then he realized that his wife had filed another complaint against him. The letter summoned him to appear at the station as soon as possible.

***

He sat in front of the interrogator, looking perfectly composed. He was used to situations like this. His wife's complaints had made him acquainted with his neighborhood police. He had many reasons to strike a pose of equanimity and solicitousness. First of all, no matter how civilized and knowledgeable he may be, Raqraq faced a hostile investigator. Secondly, this investigator was duty-bound to enforce laws designed to protect women's rights. Finally and most saliently, he knew that the interrogator would treat him as a dirty and incomprehensible Arab, even if the accused were more intellectual than the investigator's father's father.

The interrogator spent several minutes shuffling papers on his desk. It seemed that he could not find what he was looking for. Raqraq said to himself: "Do not search more, cousin, I know that you want to break my nerve with your search. We can start this investigation now, no?"

The investigator was quite young, around the same age as Husam. He opened his questioning bluntly: "Why did you threaten your wife?"

The accused placed his wounded hand on his chest and said: "I threatened her?"

"Did you not ask your twin daughters if their mother was still dancing in front of others with revealing clothes?"

As soon as Raqraq heard these words, he felt heartbreak in his throat. He did not threaten, he wanted to woo! And perhaps he hoped to relive the past out of yearning for his lost home and his beloved daughters. He looked at the investigator and insisted: "I did not threaten anyone."

"What did you do then?"

"I returned to check on people I love to make sure they are safe."

"Where do you live now? Do you live with them?"

"No, I left long ago, and I live far away."

"I understand that you exiled yourself?"

"Yes, I did." He thought to himself: "I kicked myself out or someone removed me by force, what is the difference?"

"Do you have a weapon?"

"No, I have never touched a gun."

"Do you mind if we search your home?"

"Not at all. I can accompany you there now."

"What do you do for work?"

"I am a writer, and I work for the press."

The young interrogator gestured with his hand and said: "This interrogation is over. Your words are convincing. I do not think you are a danger to anyone as long as you live away from home. There is no need to detain you."

This was the first time that Raqraq had ever met a kind investigator. It is true that outside his wife's complaints he rarely had contact with the police or investigators, except for a few occasions when he was stopped for traffic violations or because he did not cross the street using the crosswalk. The current investigator was a polite man. Raqraq thanked him and headed toward the door. As he grabbed the handle, he pictured his defiant wife, so he returned to the investigator to ask him how he could protect himself from her the next time. The young investigator whispered in his ear: "File a complaint against her. This is the only way you can protect yourself from her, and from any harm she may cause you."

Outside, a soft breeze blew into Raqraq al-Sharif's face. He said to himself: "I will not complain against her to the police. I will complain about her directly to her face." At that moment, he extended his hand in the darkness, and his owl alighted. Raqraq continued on his way, adding this episode at the police station to his strange narrative, and wondering: What story will unfold next?

As he walked toward the forest, the image of his wife, Zeina al-Sha'sha'a, and her husband, Sama'an al-Atrash, rose from the darkness of his imagination.

10

The news of Raqraq al-Sharif's release spread throughout the neighborhood like a raging fire. Finally, it stopped at the house his ex-wife shared with her play husband.

Zeina sat by herself in one corner. Sama'an could tell that something was wrong. He crossed the room, brought his face to her cheek and asked: "What annoys you?"

"Nothing."

"But everything in your face says that something is irritating you."

"It seems I've failed badly."

"Please! Speak clearly. Leave out the riddles. What prevents you from doing what you want to do?"

Zeina thought about her plan and her first husband's interference. She looked up at Sama'an and said "The little imp." Her tone was bitterness laced with frustration.

"You mean your husband, father of the newspapers?"

"Is there anyone else? Yes, him."

"Since when do you take him into consideration?"

She wanted to tell him that he did not just break into her house, he also forbid his daughters from dancing at her party of notable people. She was careful not to say too much because Sama'an, too, might get in the way. Her experience dealing with men had taught her tact. What she did say was: "You know that I don't take him into consideration. I know him as a coward who talks and does nothing. It galls me that he escaped from the police's grasp. I wanted him in prison where he couldn't come back to break in again. That illegitimate son must be backed by some people in the government. He should have been locked up for years, but somehow he leaves the police station with his head held high? So don't ask me why I am angry! My enemy is free to plot against me, and you want me to smile and laugh?"

Sama'an stretched out his hand to touch her in a lighthearted way, and Zeina's anger finally broke: "Do not tickle me," she said smiling. "This is a difficult day and I do not want to laugh."

With his eyes, Sama'an al-Atrash promised his concubine that he would fix her problems. Satisfied, Zeina gazed back as if to say, "You know that there is no voice in this neighborhood that can rise up against yours, Sama'an."

***

Zeina felt relieved. Now Raqraq was Sama'an al-Atrash's problem. It took Sama'an a long time to relax enough even just to lie down, and when he did, his bed felt like a bed of thorns. The thought of Raqraq's impudence flamed his anger into a kind of madness. The government, which beat back the surrounding nations, has failed to do anything with this cretin cockroach Raqraq al-Sharif? OK, I will show him! I will show him! I will teach him a lesson that he will never forget. If my heart hardens any more, I will throw him right out of this life. What Zeina said is true. What guarantees us that he will not break into our home again? When he returned the first time, he was weak, and it was easy to drive him out. Who can guarantee that he will stay weak? He remembered what Zeina told him, that the worthless writer may be protected by the government. Sama'an ground his false teeth so ferociously that they cracked. This did not faze him. In fact, it hardly interrupted his angry plotting. He spit out the pieces, put in another set, and talked himself from fear to resolution. The days had taught him that victory is for those who take the initiative. So how long will you wait, Sama'an the deaf? The time to act is now.

Suddenly wide awake, Sama'an strode to his closet with fresh purpose. He opened the two shutter doors, took out his yob suit, and put his helmet on his head. He headed towards the window and grabbed the pipe. Within seconds he was behind the building astride his dear friend, the motorcycle, racing through the wind and darkness. Sama'an was in a state of ecstasy—anticipated violence always made him feel this way. Exulting in his brutality, he felt that he could do whatever he wanted and that the entire world was in his grasp.

He arrived at the street near the grove where his opponents had been staying, and roared aggressively up and down the street. In his mind, he was the king of the street and no one could defy him. He felt so powerful and confident that he couldn't help but show off. He placed a small stone on the edge of the street and drove away from it. He stopped at a place where he could barely see the stone and drove his motorcycle towards it as if he were racing the wind. As he approached it, he swooped down in a tight turn, his body and bike nearly touching the ground. He grabbed the stone and sat tall on his seat, accelerating through the gust as if he himself had become the wind. Power crossed with vanity and childishness: Such was the entire scope of Sama'an's manhood manifest in his impressive but silly tricks.

As Sama'an patrolled the street, the owl watched from above. After some time, Husam emerged from the forest and entered the street.

When Sama'an saw him, he said to himself: "Now I will take the law into my own hands and execute it. I will smite you, dirty Raqraq. I will teach you to stay away forever."

Sama'an sped straight for the son of his enemy. As he drew near, he raised his front wheel high. The owl saw it all and tried to warn Husam by flying furiously through the darkness, but it was too late. Sama'an struck Husam so hard with his raised wheel that his enemy's son found himself on his back in the heart of the forest. The owl became hysterical and dove for Sama'am's eyes, pecked them out. Sama'an could do nothing to avoid the owl but fall hard to the ground.

Moments later, Sama'an came to his senses; pain surged across his body from head to toe. He looked around and saw his motorcycle wheel spinning, as if it were not quite ready for its last ride to end. Sama'an knew his motorcycle was totaled, so he left it and crawled toward the building with the red-painted stairs. It was lucky for him that he did because after he had crawled a short distance his motorcycle caught fire. The gas tank exploded with a terrific bang. He thanked God that he had crawled away in time. He had just enough strength to make it to his front door. He reached up, knocked weakly, and slumped back to the ground where Zeina found him lying in a heap. She dragged him inside and shut the door.

Zeina brought her face to his and immediately knew that he was seriously hurt and that his wounds could even be life-threatening. She asked him what happened. He told her that he wanted to save her from her husband Raqraq al-Sharif, but he was unsuccessful in accomplishing his goal, and attacked his son, Husam, instead.

Then the grieving mother shouted at him: "What? You mean you killed my son?"

He calmed her: "Do not be afraid. He is only slightly injured. I am sure he will recover quickly—much faster than I will. All I wanted was to relieve you from the everlasting intrusiveness of his mother's old lover, your husband Raqraq."

Zeina lifted Sama'an's body. With tremendous difficulty, she brought him to the inner room of her home. There, she left him resting on her bed. When she thought that he was asleep, she set out for the forest to check on her son. She crept into the heart of the forest and saw her son sitting with his father, and her mother's heart was greatly relieved.

When, on the way back, she came across the smoking wreckage of Sama'an's motorcycle, she smiled archly to herself.

11

Zeina al-Sha'sha'a returned to her house thinking about her rollercoaster day, which started with her first husband evading the police and ended with her second husband trying to kill her son. She said to herself, today is a dividing line between a dark past and a bright future. If you use your day well and use your mind as you should, then you will be lucky forever. Zeina rubbed her hands in anticipation of a bright future.

She checked the inner room where her husband was lying in pain; perhaps he is still asleep, she thought. But he was actually groaning for water. She ignored his pleading and descended the stairs with the alacrity of a butterfly that sees light glimmer through its cocoon. She walked to the side of the house, where she had forced her husband from the kitchen window, and she bent back each of the iron rods that might otherwise have rescued the next falling man.

With this precaution taken care of, Zeina returned to the inner room to look after her second husband, who lay on the bed broken and wounded. Atrash again begged for water, and this time, she brought some. As he raised his body to sip, his pain was obvious. He thanked her, and she replied: "In good health," but said to herself: "I wish it were poison. Now, I am stuck with the remains of a man who is good for nothing."

She sat on the edge of the bed assessing her husband's injuries. She touched a sensitive part of his body, but he did not move. She did it once again and again he did not move. Then, she poked a still more sensitive part, he cried out of pain and removed her hand away. These exams confirmed what Zeina saw with her eyes: Her husband is a corpse that must be buried, a body without life. What did his accident mean to Zeina? It meant that she would be a nurse to a half-dead man. She said to herself, "This will not be so."

Once she was sure that the resting man was completely incapacitated, she put her final plan into motion. She went to the kerosene fireplace in the outer room and ignited it quietly and without emotion;

she returned to the interior room and waited. The smell of the kerosene reached the nose of the exhausted man on the bed. He turned his face toward Zeina. With fear in his eyes, he said, "I am choking, where is that kerosene smell coming from?" She ignored the question and absent-mindedly tidied up the room. The heat intensified and the kerosene smell became unbearable. Sama'an started to panic. "I am suffocating! Where is this heat coming from?" The woman replied, "I do not know what you are talking about. I don't feel any heat or smell any kerosene. You must be in shock from your injuries." He pleaded with her to help him to the window. She responded: "Can't you get up yourself?" He replied by shaking his head: "Please help me." She supported his waist and he arose slowly with great effort. "I can hardly breathe. Open the window, please. Do you think my end is near?" She opened the window and reassured him in a flat voice: "God forbid, may he protect you."

The broken man hobbled to the window and leaned out, gasping for air. His wife took advantage of this moment to do what she had planned. Quickly, like someone who wants to get rid of something, Zeina grabbed his legs and flipped him out the window. Caught completely off guard, the ruined man fell headlong. Zeina looked down. She knew what the iron rods could do, but what she saw was, in fact, more horrible than she had imagined. The body of Sama'an al-Atrash was pierced by several rods, and the scene was more gruesome than any artist could create, although one could say that the scene was, indeed, the work of a masterful artist.

This artist was, of course, the very owner of the house, Zeina al-Sha'sha'a. Poor guy, he was in a motorcycle accident near the forest. His injuries were severe. He returned to the house believing that his injuries were minor, and as he rested, his body burned with pain. He went to the window to get some fresh air, he lost his balance, and he fell out. May God have mercy on him. His life ended so quickly, he had no time for farewells. Yes, yes, only a brilliant woman, like Zeina al-Sha'sha'a, could complete the first chapter of her scheme; now it was time for the second.

The owner of the house turned off the kerosene heater, put it away, and left the place as it was. Now, everything is clear, she thought. If a suspicious investigator were to ask her where she was when her injured husband fell to his death, she would tell him that she was in the forest with her son, Husam, and his father, Raqraq al-Sharif.

Zeina opened the front door and rushed down the red stairs oblivious to the darkness around her. Within moments, she was standing outside her building. After discreetly checking for potential witnesses, she hurried to the forest, careful not to seem agitated. She was in control of this narrative; she had always wanted to be the person who leads. Near the heart of the forest, she heard a conversation between her son and his father, and she was happy to see the owl sleeping in the nearby tree.

She heard the father saying: "Get ready my child. We have to visit Sama'an al-Atrash and make sure that he is well. It is true, he approached us with evil intentions. Nevertheless, we should not meet evil with evil."

Husam was not convinced. "I would rather not visit him, Dad. Without the owl's help, I would have died."

But Raqraq was adamant: "Whatever your sentiments son, we must make this visit. You heard the explosion. His injuries must be severe. He's no threat to us."

Still, Husam was not persuaded. "Unless you tell me why you are so intent on visiting our enemy, I will not leave this forest."

Raqraq obliged: "Your mother deserves to have someone standing by her side easing her grief."

But Husam stubbornly pointed out: "My mother almost imprisoned you for many years and you want to comfort her? And why would you possibly wish to visit a man who vowed to kill you and, just a few hours ago, ran over your son with his motorcycle?"

Raqraq was growing impatient. He insisted: "Come with me now, my son. Later, I will explain to you why I must visit him."

Husam again asked for an explanation, but Raqraq put him off: "Let's go now. I promise I will tell you later."

At this moment, Zeina al-Sha'sha'a appeared from behind a tree: "Tell him, tell him why you insist on visiting Sama'an al-Atrash. Tell him, I came here alone. I'd also like to know why you are planning on visiting that man. Do you miss me?"

Raqraq was shocked. He thought to himself: "What is happening today? What brought this woman here?" One thousand questions needed answers. Zeina approached the two, and the owl on the tree watched cautiously for any sign of danger. The woman looked around and said:

"You live here in this filth? Perhaps you should relocate somewhere else, anywhere but my home. The reason is simple this time: Sama'an al-Atrash has died. He felt as if he were suffocating because of his injury and went to the window. When he lost his balance, he fell to the ground where iron rods pierced his body."

The three of them—father, son, and owl—stared at her in amazement: "Is Sama'an really dead?"

Instead of answering, she replied, "I haven't come here for this reason."

The three pondered: "So, tell us why you came here to this grim forest?"

The woman responded with greater determination: "I am now preparing to carry out my plans. You have no idea what blessings God passed down when he bestowed our beloved twins on us, you do not know how much money you can make off our talented daughters in dancing and singing if they become famous. Artists today play with gold, and my daughters are just as talented as any Indian singers and Haifa Wehbe."

The father confronted her with anger: "My beloved daughters will not become a spectacle for dirty eyes."

She replied to him: "Look who is talking? You mean to tell me that you are more motherly to my beloved twins than me? By God, is the midwife more motherly than the mother?" She paused and then continued: "However, I have changed my mind. In the past, I thought of hosting a small dancing party at home attended by notables and elites."

The husband interrupted her: "Notables or yobs?"

Zeina ignored his remark: "What I want to say is that I have now decided to hold a party to announce the birth of two distinct artists: Two twins singing with one voice." She continued as if she remembered something important that she'd forgotten: "Why should this country remain barren? Why can't we produce an artist at the level as Haifa? People say that our twins look like Haifa Wehbe. Let us really try this time, we may rise from poverty. How many lives do we get to live?"

The father repeated his question: "I asked you who will attend this party? Notables of the country or yobs?"

Zeina became irritated. With anger in her voice, she asked: "Why would it be any different if we throw a big party like Haifa Wehbe and

Nancy Ajram? What do we care if this party is attended by yobs and bitches? Our girls have talent, and this is how you break into the business!"

The father looked towards his son Husam and said to his former wife: "There is no way that my sweethearts will show up in the theater half-naked like Haifa and others."

Zeina's patience was at its limit. Her blood pressure rose in her veins and she replied: "Listen to me. That's enough! You are making yourself out to be a sheikh and a monk now? I am telling you that we will not throw a party in our house, but we will hold a concert that can be attended by anyone. And you challenge me on this? Listen! I am telling you that we will hold an event to showcase the talent of our unique twins. Their voices will light up this devastated neighborhood, blighted by poverty and bereft of art. You say that you don't want your daughters to wear revealing clothes. Excuse me from the nonsense of your closed-mindedness! Open your mind to the possibilities! Do you see where the world is and where we are now? Is your only desire to stay poor? Leave our God alone, look to yourself, you are chasing newspapers and books and our lives are miserable. You are powerless to bestow mercy on us, and you don't want mercy bestowed on us by others!"

The father's anger rose as he said: "Where do these words come from? All I am saying is that I do not want licentiousness to infect my family. You are duplicitous! If our twins were talented in dancing and singing, we would have seen the signs by now. The real artist doesn't suddenly appear. Let's take for example the star of *Arab Idol*, Muhammad A'ssaf. He started singing in the streets of the camp as a little boy. In the end, I want to tell you: I do not want divorced twins. Most artists fail in their married lives. In my opinion, a woman in her home is better than a divorced artist."

The mother clapped in his face: "Have you finished your precious lecture? Are you through with your nonsense? I will hold this showcase! My girls will be famous artists, divorced or not. We will all bathe in money. Let them get divorced. What bad would happen to them? These days divorced women live better lives than most married women."

The father finally lost his patience: "My daughters will not be divorced from their husbands as long as I live!"

Now, Zeina started writing the final chapter of her plan. She directed her words to her husband and said: "What if I told you that you killed Sama'an al-Atrash, and I witnessed it with my own eyes, which will one day be eaten by worms in my grave? What would you say then?"

These unexpected words surprised the stubborn interlocutor. After stammering and stalling, he blurted out: "What are you saying, you're saying that I killed him?"

"Yes, you killed him. Everyone knows you've wanted him dead since you discovered him living at home with your wife! But he was too strong. You took advantage of his injuries and threw him from the window of his house."

Having played her trump, she showed Raqraq her back and walked briskly away. But after a few steps, she turned to say: "Don't forget, you are accused of murder. We'll see if the government will protect you now."

She took a few more steps, turned again, and added confidently: "You have two options: You can agree to this showcase—I don't care if my daughters get a divorce—or you will find yourself accused of murdering your ex-wife's husband."

And with that, Zeina left all those present, including the owl, to contemplate their predicament.

12

The music from the house of twin daughters Rafiqa and Shafiqa could be heard a kilometer away. Visitors enjoyed a remarkable scene. The homemakers wore tiger-print dresses that clung tightly to their full bodies, and their mother sat high in a chair. In her bosom was a durbaka that she beat with skillful hands, hands that were anxious for wealth and eminence. The twins were shaking their breasts and dancing so enticingly that they could excite even stone itself. The smoke of countless cigarettes thickened the air. When the two girls stopped momentarily to rest, their mother urged them to continue:

"Where is the singing? I want to see dancing and singing fit to enliven the neighborhood from border to border." She shot her two daughters a stern look: "I want movement. I want sensuousness. Have you not seen how Haifa makes the crowds go wild just by moving her hips?"

To make her point, Zeina put the durbaka aside and leapt to the middle of the room. She began to gesture with her hands and shake her breasts seductively: "This is dancing, it does not matter what the song lyrics mean. It is important to be sensuous like the words, 'I love you.'"

She returned to her seat and embraced her durbaka again: "Let's continue the exercise. The party date is approaching, and we must have an event that will be remembered for ages to come. This is the first step to fame and money."

Just as the twin sisters had finally begun dancing and singing as their mother had instructed—that is, once they had learned to shake their bottoms with sufficient abandon—their twin husbands entered the room. The dancing sisters caught sight of their husbands and immediately stopped dancing. Their mother continued beating the durbaka unaware. When she finally noticed her sons-in-law, she tried to soothe them with an exaggerated show of respect: "Welcome, my respectable sons-in-law."

They ignored the insincere welcome and asked in one voice: "What is this noise?"

The two wives withdrew in a hurry, looking like confused tigers. The mother rushed in to save the situation, calmly explaining: "The party is approaching, and we must prepare for it. The time of the improvised performance has past. Whoever wants to be an artist in our time must be prepared. One must train to succeed. I hope you know that success doesn't come easily."

Each husband shot a meaningful glance to his wife and her alluring dress, and said in an angry voice: "Who told you that we permitted our wives to participate in this farce of a party?"

The mother-in-law felt her control of the scene start to slip, so she shifted gears and tried her form of reason: "Why not participate? Life has become difficult today, and if one does not try to advance oneself, man or woman, there is no future. What harm would it bring if your wives became famous stars? Women of the Owl Neighborhood do not deserve to have bright stars in their midst? Isn't it better to be famous than to be another anonymous woman busy with cooking, only raising children, and choking in poverty?"

The mother uttered these last words in a slow and measured voice. Ostensibly, she aimed her words at the husbands, but her two daughters were her real targets: "The time of the imprisoned woman in the house has ended. Women want challenging lives, and we demand our full rights and freedoms. We want dignity and equality. Husbands have to help their wives get these things instead of frustrating us in dead-end lives."

Well aware of their slippery mother-in-law's tricks, the angry husbands bristled: "Are you threatening us?"

The mother-in-law motioned as if this question, at once, pleased and displeased her: "I didn't threaten anyone, God forbid! All I want is to bring happiness to your home, my home and the Owl Neighborhood."

The two opened their eyes together and wondered aloud in one voice: "Do we understand correctly that you expect our wives to practice dancing and singing for that damned party you are throwing?"

Zeina's expression changed all at once. She responded dismissively: "Understand whatever you want. The party will be held as scheduled. It's going to happen, and we'll keep training."

The twin husbands looked at each other in disbelief, shocked that their mother-in-law's boldness could rise to the point of provoking them in their own homes: "What are you really saying? And what if we told you that we won't allow this dancing in our home. What would you say then?"

The mother-in-law coolly shrugged her shoulders in mockery and contempt: "Of course, I will not occupy your home by force, we'll not train ourselves here by force."

She stopped in the middle of the room like someone ending a phone call that had gotten on her nerves, and pointed at her two daughters, asking them to pack as much clothing as they needed until the party date a few days away. The two sisters were surprised at their mother's request and did not move until Zeina repeated her order more forcefully.

As one, the two daughters disappeared into their rooms. They had no choice but to obey their mother. Filial obedience is a must in all religions. After a short time, they returned—each holding a travel handbag in a tiger print that matched her dress. They looked to their husbands to gauge their reactions and were surprised to hear them asking: "Where are you going?"

They looked at their mother and saw her waiting near the door. She winked at them, encouraging them to comply. The women answered by appeasing their mother: "Where do you think, to Taluzah city? We are going with our mother to our home. We must continue practicing. If this house cannot accommodate our ambitions, we will return to our old house."

Flustered almost beyond speech, the husbands asked their wives one last time: "Do we understand that you are ignoring us and that you have decided to perform without even asking us, as if we are unimportant men of no status."

The mother-in-law and her daughters were not cowed. To the contrary, they spoke firmly: "Understand whatever you want. The party will go on, meaning we will continue practicing. No one can deter us from our plans."

The three women turned to the door and left.

The angry husbands confirmed the women were outside and went up to the roof, and yelled to their wives: "You are divorced!" The twin daughters followed their mother without breaking stride. A short while ago, they were two wives walking behind their divorced mother. Now they are three women, a mother and her two daughters, sharing the status of divorcee.

13

The three women left their husbands in a maze of questions. What happened? Why couldn't we have defused the situation? Wasn't there some way to stop her? No. No, we could not have simply expelled this crazy woman from our home. She is their mother, after all. And she brainwashed her daughters. She convinced them that a wonderful artistic duo would soon be born and immediately catch the eye of bigshots in the entertainment business. They were told that the Owl Neighborhood had never witnessed such artists in its history. But we, their husbands, were never so much as consulted. Our wives carried out the worst schemes of that woman's desperate and sick imagination. Had she no idea that her mania would destroy two houses and add two new names to the list of Owl Neighborhood divorcees?

The two brothers sat alone in their homes for the first time in a long time. Yes, it is true that they were once used to this solitude, but since they had found their purpose in their twin brides their lives had changed, leaving loneliness behind forever, or so they thought.

Each brother went to his closet and grabbed his photo album and looked through pictures taken in different parts of the world. Hours and hours passed as the lonely brothers slowly turned the pages, each one in his way remembering and yearning for his wife. How many beautiful places we visited together! Few people in the Owl Neighborhood had known such happy married life. And here, in this same neighborhood, we found its sad end.

"We shouldn't have acted so hastily. If we had responded in a more measured way, this wouldn't have happened, and we could continue our happy lives." These words of regret hung in the air for what seemed like hours. But after a time, one of the brothers said what was on both of their minds: "Why did we allow that woman, our mother-in-law, to control our household and do us like she did her polite husband, the storyteller?" The two formed a sad tableau, sitting absolutely still, each with an album on his lap opened to pictures of his wife, or ex-wife.

Finally, out of the gloom, an idea occurred to both brothers at once: "Why don't we go to our father-in-law in the forest and speak with him? Didn't he promise to tell us one of his stories?"

For the first time in hours, the brothers moved. In minutes, they were outside walking swiftly toward the forest.

***

Under a tall tree, in the heart of the forest, the father Raqraq al-Sharif sat on the ground with his son Husam. Above them, on a nearby branch, the owl stood watch, wondering: Why do they sit facing away from each other? What's going on? What's the meaning of this?

After all he had been through, Raqraq was melancholy and tired. His words matched his pensive mood: "I think we have to start over," he told his son. "The wonderful times with loved ones go by quickly. They are like evaporating water. When they are gone, it is as if they did not exist, except as a fantasy that once lived in our minds and nowhere else. I want you to remember that I did not neglect anyone from my dear family. Your mother insisted on setting up that dance party for your sisters. Of course, I opposed it, but you were here and saw and heard what she said. I feel now, exactly as I felt on that distant day, when I left our home the first time. That was a long time ago. I felt like an empty vessel. I could not do anything those days, and even if I could have, I wouldn't have. You know I am a rational man. And I knew the law well. It says that you cannot force anyone, even your kids, to do as you please. Your child is free to do whatever he wants, especially if he is of age."

Husam was confused by his father's digression. "I know, Father," he said, "but why the sad speech?"

"Wait, my son. Do not be hasty. Hastiness always loses. Let me finish. This meeting may be our last. Soon, I will be on my way there, to the unknown. I want you to be strong, not weak. Deal with life with your mind, not just with passion. I am telling you these words because I do not want you to live the same way that I did, to be isolated in your home and to feel lonely among your own children."

Raqraq's solemn words troubled his son. "Do not say this, Father, you are hurting me."

But the father continued, "You know, my son, I was a peaceful man all my life. I avoided evil all the time, but evil follows me everywhere I go. I do not want what happened to me to happen to you. I want you to be strong and happy."

Husam could not find the words to reply, so the two sat in silence under the great tree, and the owl stood guard. They were quiet a long time when, suddenly, a distant sound caught the attention of the father, the son and the owl. They stared into the darkness, compelled to discover its source. "Who is there?" Raqraq yelled. A moment later, he was surprised to make out the twin husbands of his daughters. Pleased by this unexpected reunion, the father greeted them heartily. When the thrill of meeting had faded, the men reflected on their strange predicament. Fittingly, Raqraq spoke first: "I returned to the neighborhood to be once again part of a loving family. Unfortunately, what I wanted has hit an impasse in this new era of imported laws. Who would have thought years ago that such an encounter as this would warm my heart?"

The twin brothers asked: "What do you mean, my uncle?"

Raqraq pointed to the forest surrounding them: "I mean, we live in different circumstances than our cousins who lived in Europe, so we faced and still face difficulties in accepting laws that pay no mind to our traditions and values. In any case, we live in a time of transition, and someone has to pay the price. I do not believe that any Arab house will be spared these changes. The pain of transformation will enter our houses one by one, and it will drive a wedge between many husbands and their wives, and it will alienate many children from their parents."

The writer paused, as if to gather his thoughts, then continued: "The laws, which are implemented in this country, regarding our home life, especially the women's protection law, are products of Europe. These laws are good for Europe, but they do not fit our culture."

He directed his words to his sons-in-law, wondering aloud: "Which good wind brought you?"

The sons-in-law smiled: "It's the same wind that you talk about, the wind of change that leaves no sanctuary for the Arab family in this country."

The grieving father asked: "Did you divorce your wives?"

The two shook their heads in sorrow, and their father-in-law said to them, "I expected this a long time ago. Whoever has a mother-in-law in sympathy with the recent laws has to pay a very steep price. And where are your wives now?"

The two replied: "Their mother is determined to hold this party for them. She took them with her."

The tormented father looked into the distance and said: "Woe to us in this country. Our women have become our adversaries. Yesterday, my wife was the number one woman in my life, and she has become my number one enemy."

He looked to his sons-in-law and asked: "What do you intend to do now?"

They answered together: "This is why we came, we want your advice."

The father said: "Leave things as they are, maybe your days will bring unexpected news. What we are incapable of doing, the days will do, and they will offer it to us on a plate of joy."

The sons-in-law smiled: "This is exactly what we will do, my uncle."

***

Raqraq al-Sharif looked closely at his surroundings, as if he wanted to carve a place for them in his heart. He focused his gaze on his son Husam and thought: Oh God, life is very short. Yesterday, Husam was born and today he is a young man. It is comforting that the father should leave behind him a son in this life. Raqraq looked intently at his son and experienced that fleeting moment that can never be repeated.

Husam went to his father and hugged him with infinite affection and said: "Where will you go, my Father, in this dark night?"

The father said sadly: "My days in this world have ended. I must return to the other world, into the unknown, where my friends await me."

The father embraced his sons-in-law. He wished for them to go back to their homes and to their wives, his daughters. Then he approached the owl and stretched out his hand, and she perched there. He looked at her with affection like a father who knows the deep meaning of father-hood: "Come on, my owl, come on, I will take you there with me. To my other home, you'll be the link that connects the worlds."

With that Raqraq al-Sharif went on his way. The deeper he jour-neyed into the darkness, the farther behind he left his sorrow. In the final moment before he disappeared forever, Husam ran after him to say one last thing, but the darkness swallowed Raqraq before his son could speak, so the final words never left Husam's mouth. Were those words: "I promise, my Father, to preserve everything beautiful you left behind?" Maybe ... Perhaps ... Who knows?

CPSIA information can be obtained
at www.ICGtesting.com
Printed in the USA
BVHW091236190921
617061BV00017BA/1397